HOW MUCH BIG IS THE SKY

A MEMOIR OF A MOTHER'S LOVE AND UNFATHOMABLE LOSS

SHERRY CHAPMAN

PEDIGREE PUBLISHING

Copyright © 2019 by Sherry Chapman

All rights reserved. No part of this book may be reproduced in any form or by any electronic or mechanical means, including information storage and retrieval systems, without written permission from the author, except for the use of brief quotations in a book review.

Published by Pedigree Publishing, Coventry, Connecticut, U.S.A.

For discounts on bulk purchases or information on how to schedule an event with the author, contact Pedigree Publishing at info@pedigreepublishing.com.

This is a work of nonfiction. In some cases, names have been changed to protect and respect the privacy of others.

The "In Memoriam" poems that launch each of the five parts of this book were previously published in the *Hartford Courant*.

Used with permission and grateful acknowledgment are:

"Ryan," the poem read at the cemetery service, © 2002 by Chris Peck.

"In Memoriam," introduction to Part III: Yearning and Isolation, © 2003 by Amber LaChappelle.

Cover design by 100covers.

Author photograph by Laura Stone Photography.

Library of Congress Control Number: 2019912836

ISBN: 978-1-951307-01-1 (hc)

ISBN: 978-1-951307-02-8 (pbk)

ISBN: 978-1-951307-00-4 (e-bk)

For my son, Ryan Aaron Ramirez
and
Josh Rogers, Adrian Soares,
Daniel Palmer, Joey DuMouchel,
Steven LaChappelle, Dominic Pruneau,
Billy Tedford, Beulah E. Baughman,
Edward Donald Tomlin, Wendy Walker Lopes, Brendon Lastrina,
Brandon Reeve, Eric Kalber, Alexander Bousquet, Reid Hollister,
Alyssa Roy, Adrian Podbielski, Anthony Apruzzese,
Jessica Apruzzese, Viviana Cavalli, Lauren Bedell,
John Hawkes Marvin, James Christopher Marvin, Benjamin Daub,
Donald Orange II, Oliver Ciparelli, Noelle Starr Arpin,
Lucille Rose LaChappelle, Timothy John Lally,
Dustin Paolino, Ellen Pasay,
and
all the other children and young adults that we lost too soon.

A shadow flits before me,
Not thou, but like to thee;
Ah Christ, that it were possible
For one short hour to see
The souls we loved, that they might tell us
What and where they be!

— ALFRED, LORD TENNYSON

CONTENTS

PART I
SHOCK AND DENIAL   1

PART II
YEARNING AND ISOLATION   71

PART III
PURPOSE AND FRENZY   167

PART IV
REFLECTION   221

PART V
RESIGNATION   265

Acknowledgments   300
Reading Group Questions   302

PART I
SHOCK AND DENIAL

In Memoriam

She sang her baby a lullaby;
she soothed her son so he would not cry.
She held him close.

She steadied his hand
as he learned how to walk;
chased a tottering bike
as he learned how to ride.
She kissed his scrapes.

She sat in fields and gymnasiums
through games and tournaments
cheering him on in play and competition.
She was his fan.

She grilled all his fish catches,
no matter how bony,
and with hardly a detectable grimace,
she ate his fish.

She watched as he grew,
maturing and handsome;
her pride was apparent,
her work almost done.
She was his mom.

She sang her baby a lullaby,
as she beseeched the Heavens
not to let her son die.
She held him close.

THE PHONE CALL

*S*omething tugs at me in the distance as a part of an unsettling dream. I turn into Michael and wrap a leg over his. He folds his body just right to accommodate mine, like the perfect dance. He rests a hand on my thigh. I doze off again.

My eyes snap awake with the ringing. I push myself up to peer over Michael at the illuminated numbers of the clock on his side of the bed. I have to squint my left eye to get rid of the blur. The clock glares back at me: 4:12 A.M. *Something is wrong.*

The phone rings again and Michael gives me a pat on the leg that I recognize as encouragement. It could not be more obvious. "Thanks for handling this while I continue to sleep," his touch says.

Tossing the comforter aside, I gulp down a panicked heartbeat and confront the blanket of chill head-on. It takes me five strides to reach the phone, shrieking now, on the dresser against the wall opposite the bed.

"Hello?" Tentative.

"Mrs. Chapman?"

I don't answer fast enough.

"Are you Ryan's mom?" the woman on the other end of the line asks.

"Yes." Dread combined with something like electricity courses through my body.

"I'm calling from Hartford Hospital." My stomach plunges into some nether space.

"No." It's the only word I can form.

"Ryan was in a car accident." Bile rises in my throat. I have to swallow before I can speak again.

"Is he okay?" *Please be okay. Please be okay. Please be okay.*

"It's serious," she says. "He's with the trauma team right now." The echo of my heart pounds through my ears like a frantic knock on the door.

"But will he be okay?" I'm begging now. *Please tell me he'll be okay. Please.*

"It's very serious," she says.

I hear myself whimpering and then the click of a switch. Michael's reading light illuminates the bedroom. He grabs his shirt from the nearby chair, pulls it over his head. He mouths a "What?" to me as he gets up to retrieve his jeans from the top of the trunk at the foot of the bed.

The woman on the phone tells me to be careful driving to the hospital. "It's dangerous out there," she says. "The roads are very slick and icy."

I drop the phone. "Ryan," I say, finally answering Michael. "Hartford Hospital." It's all I can manage between the gulping and the gasping. I'm trying to keep my stomach in place. Trying to keep my heart from hurtling out of my chest.

"It's serious," I add, rushing to the closet to get dressed. My fingers don't work right and it takes too long to button my flannel shirt. I can't find my other boot. I hold back a scream.

EVERY PARENT'S NIGHTMARE

The terror has settled in my throat.

"What happened?" Michael asks.

"Car crash," I gulp. Monosyllables are the best I can do. My stomach is a butter churn. Something threatens to burst out of my skull. The rush of it is in my ears. I press my left hand to the top of my head to keep it in.

I gasp for breath throughout the thirty-five-minute ride to the hospital, clutching the passenger-side armrest as tightly as I can. The Nissan Xterra crawls along ice-slick, snow-banked streets and highways while every particle in my body moves at lightning speed.

Michael stops at the emergency entrance. It takes a precious second to loosen my frozen grip on the armrest and open the car door. I charge into the emergency room as Michael drives away to find a place to park.

A woman sitting behind a desk looks up.

"We got a call. My son is here. Ryan."

"Ryan who? Can you spell that?" *Oh, my God.* "We have no record—"

"But someone called us from here." The fear is wedged in my

stomach now, my heart hammering percussion. Michael touches my right elbow to let me know he's joined me.

"Why was he—"

"Car crash."

She signals the security guard. Does he know anything? Nope. She makes phone calls. We wait. I plead with a God I want to believe in. *Please, God, please, God,* filling my head so other thoughts can't settle. The fear grips me like a strangle-hold, as if two giant hands are squeezing my entire body as hard as they can.

A phone call, a teenager's life hanging in the balance. Surely, they expected us. *Maybe he—no.* I push the thought from my head before it has a chance to fully form. *Please, God, please, God.* My silent mantra.

"Found him!" the receptionist shouts out to us. "He's in an operating room."

I almost fall to the floor as the giant hands release me and a surge of some softer thing, relief, takes hold.

"He's alive then," I say. "He's alive."

The receptionist directs us to the elevator bank. "Go up to the fifth floor," she says. "There's a waiting area. Someone will be with you shortly."

The chime of the elevator announces we have reached the fifth floor. The doors open to a hallway, with an exposed waiting area just beyond. Two women who've been thrust into some other horror greet us only with their eyes. They are huddled together on a seat in the far left corner. Michael leads me to one of the nearest seats on the right, a chair diagonally opposite the women. They speak in hushed whispers. Michael and I don't talk. *He's alive,* I say to myself. *He's alive.* The industrial-looking wall clock above the elevator door broadcasts the time as 4:59 A.M.

I look at the clock again after staring at the floor for what feels like forever. 5:02.

Turning to Michael, "I wonder how long—"

"I don't know," he answers. "She said shortly."

Every wire holding the pieces of me together is supercharged. I stand up and pace from one end of the waiting area to the other, trying to manage my inner turmoil. *He's alive, please, God, he's alive, please, God*—each word measured with a footstep. I pace and pace as time moseys along one prolonged second after another. Michael sits, stands, walks, sits again. He reaches out to me and I shrug him off. I can't stop the pleading or the pacing.

When six o'clock rolls around, we go searching—down hallways, through doors, around corners. We find a nurses' station.

"Can you help us? We're looking for our son. Ryan."

A woman in scrubs makes a phone call. She turns her back to us. The conversation is hushed.

"Go back to the waiting area," she says. "Someone will be with you shortly."

RYAN

If you don't go into labor in the next few days, we'll have to induce," the obstetrician said. The baby should have been born already.

"I can schedule you for this Friday, the 18th, or Monday, the 21st. Do you have a preference?"

"November 18," I said with a smile. "It's my birthday."

Still pregnant when Friday arrived, I gave my three-year-old daughter Amber a kiss, a hug, and a promise. She would join me at the hospital later that day to meet her baby brother or sister.

I left Amber in the care of my grandmother while my aunt drove me to the hospital. The children's biological father and I had permanently separated early in my pregnancy. I'd grown strong in the preceding months. I would have this baby on my own.

"I'm told it's your birthday," the ultrasound technician said.

"Yup, twenty-six now. An old lady."

She grinned, running the ultrasound wand over my exposed abdomen. "You're getting an extra special present today."

"I can't think of a better gift," I laughed.

"Do you want to know the gender?"

I thought about that for a moment. If it was a boy, his name would be Ryan. If it was a girl, her name would be Autumn. "No," I replied. "I've waited this long."

"Surprise me, little one," I said to my belly.

They brought me to a delivery room, attached monitoring sensors to my abdomen, and induced me through an IV in my arm. A machine measured the baby's heart rate and my contractions with lines on a screen and corresponding bleeps.

"Don't forget to take lots of pictures," I told one of the nurses. Since I was alone, the responsibility of the first baby pictures ended up in the hands of a nurse whose name would be lost to history.

They peppered me with words of support and encouragement. Over time, the contractions became more pronounced, more difficult to bear.

I may have been slow to recognize the concerned activity in the room. Elevated voices sandwiched between whispers.

"What's wrong?" I asked. "Is something wrong?"

My obstetrician walked the few steps from the monitoring machine to the gurney. "Your contractions are compressing his heart," he said.

It registered immediately that the doctor said "his" heart. *Oh*, I thought to myself, *it's a boy then*.

"Is he okay?"

"We need to perform an emergency cesarean section," he said, avoiding my question. I noticed the perspiration on his upper lip. He turned to address the other medical personnel. "Now," he snapped.

Everyone seemed to have a specific task, unhooking me from or hooking me up to various apparatus.

"We need to get you to the OR," a nurse explained.

"But is my baby okay?"

"We'll do the best we can."

"But . . ." I stopped, trembling as the panic set in, realizing I was asking for assurances they couldn't give. I wanted to tell them how much I already loved this child. How nothing could be wrong because we needed him. How he was already a part of our family. But all I could say, and it came out in a whisper, was, "Ryan." Then, "My son." The first time in my life I had combined those words.

"His name is Ryan," I said more forcefully so that everyone in the room would hear his name.

The nurse looked down at me and I saw the warmth and compassion in the folds of her faded denim-blue eyes. She patted my arm.

"We're gonna do everything we can, honey."

"My daughter," I said, needing her to understand. "She's three. I promised her she'd meet the baby today."

The nurse touched my cheek and turned away.

They wheeled me into a room where I met the anesthesiologist, who was older than I expected and a little unsteady in my opinion. *Doesn't this require some precision?* I wondered as he explained the procedure that would block the pain of the cesarean birth. I wished I hadn't caught sight of the needle. About a foot long, I guessed. I tried not to focus on the tremble in his hands.

"Do it," I told him after he announced he was ready to proceed. We had to get my son delivered safely.

I sat on the operating room table, legs dangling over the side, upper body hunched forward as much as possible given the size of my belly. The backside of my gown was open, exposing my lower spine to the trembling man with the big needle. "But please be careful," I added.

I was careful myself. Steady during the injection, which was timed between contractions. Careful to hold my eyes open. Careful not to breathe, so that not even a blink or a breath would interfere with his concentration.

All that carefulness paid off. A short time later I was strapped down on my back with a sheeted screen over my chest, which blocked my view of what was happening to the lower two-thirds of my body. Not the natural birth I had hoped for.

"It's a boy!" a woman whose voice I didn't recognize announced from behind the screen. Someone held Ryan up so I could see him, but just briefly. He had a shock of dark hair. I listened for a cry that didn't come. I heard a lot of movement.

"Can I hold him?" I asked.

"Let's get you stitched up first," the obstetrician said.

"Is he okay?" I asked, still waiting for that cry.

"He's being evaluated right now."

"But is he okay?" No answer.

They settled me into a room of my own on the maternity ward.

"Where's my son?" I kept asking until eventually I shouted it through my tears and fatigue. "Where—is—my—son?" Too much time had passed with no explanation.

"Shhh," a woman in nursing scrubs said. "You're upsetting the other women on the ward." She raised the head of my bed, gave me a pill and a sip of water, handed me some Kleenex.

"I'm scared," I said, wiping my face. "I need to talk to the doctor."

As if I had summoned him, he was at the door.

"What's wrong?" I asked him.

He looked tired and worried. "There are some complications."

"What?"

"He was born with a collapsed lung."

"But . . . is that treatable?" I asked.

"And he is exhibiting symptoms . . ."

I realized I was holding my breath as he paused.

"His symptoms are consistent with those of babies born without kidneys."

"What does that mean?"

"Babies without kidneys cannot survive." He took a deep

13

breath. "We're emergency transporting him to John Dempsey Neonatal Intensive Care where he'll undergo additional testing."

"Can I see him? I need to see him."

"He's in an incubator. You won't be able to hold him."

"I just want to see him."

A short time later, they rolled the incubator close to my hospital bed. There was nothing covering Ryan except for the tape that held the tubes protruding from his arms and orifices. Pain was on his face. I could see it in the wrinkle of his brow, in the twist of his mouth. But he was silent.

Stoic, I thought. *He's a stoic little boy.* He looked slight and undernourished. His ribs protruded. He had dark hair and dark eyes that were visible through a sliver of a squint. I wanted to comfort him, to hold him. The longing was so great that my chest ached.

"Can't I hold him?" I pled through my tears.

"We have to go," one of the transporting attendants responded. Two of them were in the hospital room, along with the doctor and the woman in scrubs.

Despite the wound extending from one side of my swollen tummy to the other, I managed to place my face up against the incubator. "Hi, Ryan. It's mommy," I said, leaving tear smudges and kiss marks on the glass so that a piece of me would travel with him. I held back a sob as I said, "I'm sorry this is your first view of the world. Mommy loves you."

Through staggered breath, I sang to him. "Hush little baby, don't you cry . . ." I inspected every visible inch of his body through the barrier. There was a cut on his head.

"What happened to his head?" I looked up at the doctor.

"That's a birth injury," he said. "It's superficial."

I didn't give voice to my thoughts. That they cut his little head when they made the incision that brought him into this world. *My poor baby.*

Ryan was squirming under the bright light shining down on him from the upper part of the incubator.

"Can you turn the light off?" I asked.

"Well, don't you want to be able to see him?"

"It bothers him." I already knew my baby boy. "It's too bright. Can you turn it off?"

Now I realize the light was probably needed to keep Ryan warm. Regardless, an attendant switched it off. Then they took Ryan away, and I didn't think to ask if I could go with him.

The hospital staff kept me sedated to keep me quiet. When I wasn't in a drug-induced sleep or stupor, I was disruptive, either bawling or asking for answers. It wasn't a proper fit. Me on a maternity ward with happy new mothers and healthy new babies. They found a room for me at the far end of the hall.

Someone gave me the phone number of the intensive care unit Ryan was in. I called more often than they liked. I interrogated the obstetrician.

"You said he *may not* have kidneys?"

"His symptoms are consistent with that."

"So, he may *have* kidneys?"

"It's possible something else is going on."

"When will I know?"

"Monday."

"Why not sooner?"

"We couldn't schedule the testing until Monday."

"But there is the ultrasound. Can't you tell if he has kidneys by looking at the ultrasound?"

"It's not conclusive."

On Tuesday, I learned Ryan was fine. He had kidneys, his collapsed lung was healing, and he would not have any lingering problems. I had difficulty believing this—two such opposing diagnoses in less than a week.

"What happened then?" I asked the obstetrician. What I learned was that since Ryan was overdue, my placenta had stopped nourishing him, which is why he was so thin at birth. Much of my amniotic fluid was lost over time in undetectable increments, so there was little to cushion Ryan from the contractions. My contractions were blocking the blood flow through the placenta, interfering with his heartbeat, collapsing his lung, requiring the emergency cesarean. Ryan may not have survived if he had been born a generation earlier.

On Tuesday evening, we celebrated. My aunt, who I had christened as "Ant" Shirley in a letter I wrote to her when I was seven, brought Amber and the rest of the family to the hospital. I got out of bed for the occasion.

"Mommy!" Amber wrapped her arms around one of my legs.

"Hi my little bright spot!" I wanted to pick her up but couldn't lift anything yet, so I bent to kiss the top of her head and caress the length of her blond hair. "I missed you."

"Me too," she muffled in my leg.

I raised her chin so that she was looking at my face and kissed the air above her. "I love you."

"Me too," Amber said.

It was the first time we were together since Ryan's birth. Amber and I had never been apart for more than a few hours in the three and one-quarter years of her life. Although we had talked on the phone every morning and evening, it was a traumatic time apart. Amber perked up during the celebratory hospital dinner. I had to unzip myself from her when it was time to go.

"I'll be home in two days, Amber." I held up two fingers. "Tomorrow is day one." I dropped my middle finger. "And the next day is day two." I dropped my index finger. "I'll be home the day after tomorrow."

"With my little bwotha!" Amber exclaimed. She hadn't yet learned to enunciate the letter "r".

"Yup." I smiled and wondered why it hadn't occurred to me before now that Amber would not be able to pronounce her brother's name. She referred to herself as "Amba," and now I realized Ryan would be "Wyan" for some indefinite period of time.

∼

Ryan was healthy enough to rejoin me the following day. He was discharged and transported by ambulance from the neonatal intensive care unit at John Dempsey Hospital that morning.

A nurse I hadn't seen during my six-day stay handed me the swaddled little bundle of a boy. It was an awkward exchange.

"Do you always hold him like that?" she asked.

I felt a little testy. She had handed Ryan to me in a way that caused me to hold him in my right arm like a football, his head nestled in the crook of my elbow, his bottom in the palm of my hand.

"It's the first time I've held him," I responded, staring at Ryan's perfect little sleeping face, trying to make the appropriate adjustments without disturbing him. It's not like I didn't know how to hold a baby. He was my second after all. But maneuvering Ryan over the incision that stretched across the lower part of my stomach presented a challenge.

"Here," her voice was softer as she plucked Ryan from my arm with her thick, brown capable hands and flipped him so his head lay against my breast, his body now supported by my left arm.

"There you go," she said.

Once I had Ryan back, I held him every waking moment, trying to make up for lost time. Re-familiarizing him with the beat of his mama's heart. Giving him the sustenance he didn't get those last days in the womb, those first days following his birth.

They released us from the hospital twenty-four hours later, Ryan cradled in a protective maternal hug. *You're safe now,* I promised him.

It was Thanksgiving Day.

GREAT EXPECTATIONS

*A*s instructed for the second time, Michael and I wind our way back to the fifth floor waiting area. The two women are still sitting in those same seats. It isn't long before we hear footsteps coming toward us from down the hall. We turn our heads to study one another. I check the clock. 6:10 A.M. Two people in medical scrubs approach. A man and a woman.

"Chapman family?" the man asks. He must be the surgeon. Hopeful and expectant, we search his face.

"Yes. Is Ryan okay?" Finally, the news we have been waiting for.

"I'm sorry," he says.

"No."

"We couldn't save him."

"No." I'm helpless to do anything but deny it. Shaking my head to rid it of his words. "No. No. No. No."

"He rallied there for a while. I thought—"

My knees buckle. Michael grabs for me in slow motion as I collapse. He makes strange gasping sounds that turn into sobs. I can't hear the rest of the man's words over Michael's cries and the chaos in my body and the sensation of the cool floor on my cheek. I am paralyzed. The world turns dark.

FAMILY ROOM

We are brought to a place in the hospital they call the Family Room, where they take parents whose children have died. A nurse is talking about her teenage son, how she worries. A welcome ocean wave pounds in my head drowning her out—trying to be polite while silently repeating another mantra—*please stop, please stop, please*. I can't bear to hear about her nineteen-year-old son, who is alive. I hug myself, rocking back and forth. Michael sits close on my right, his left hand at my lower back.

"Amber," I say turning to Michael. We need to tell her. "And Kalum," I add, wondering how you inform an almost-three-year-old boy that his only uncle is dead. Michael seems to understand my unspoken concerns. He nods.

People sit with us, walk in and out and back in again. First, that female nurse with the teenage son, and then a male nurse, stout and cropped, and then the matronly chaplain.

"Do you have any questions?" The female nurse turns the discussion away from her son who worries her so.

"Was anyone with him?" My voice has no force, no louder than a whisper.

"Yes, two people."

"Who? Are they okay?"

"I can't give you their names," she says. "One is doing fine. The other is still being evaluated, but his injuries aren't life-threatening."

"Who was driving?"

"We don't know."

"What type of vehicle were they in?"

"We don't have that information."

"How was Ryan transported?"

"By ambulance." She pauses, looks at the floor and more somberly says, "LIFE STAR was grounded."

Oh, God, LIFE STAR could have saved him.

The door slams open. One of Ryan's best friends, Patrick, crashes in, wild, followed by Melissa.

"Is he okay?"

Michael shakes his head. I'm slow to respond.

Their matching orange jackets remind me that Ryan wants a nice down-filled jacket for Christmas.

"Orange?" I had asked him. Ryan answered with a wide grin, showing off the perfect smile that five years of orthodontics bought us.

"No," he chuckled. "Definitely not orange."

I stare at the sway of Melissa's long wheat-blond hair. I can't look into the sapphire of her eyes. I can't bring myself to look Pat in the face either.

"He's dead," I say, not knowing how else to convey it. Now that the words are out, I glance up at Pat, towering above us. I see his face collapse before he bursts into tears. As one, Pat and Melissa drop onto the empty sofa. Pat cries huge retching gulps. Melissa leans into him and whispers in his ear.

So, Ryan wasn't with Pat and Melissa. They're okay. It's like a puzzle, piecing this together.

∼

I can't push the surgeon's words out of my head. "He rallied there for a while." That must mean Ryan fought very hard. He wanted to live. He almost did live. The realization that Ryan was alive while we paced in the waiting area hits me like a body slam. I could have held him and told him how much I love him. I could have told him to hold on, to fight harder, that I can't live without him. It might have been enough. But the possibilities are lost forever now.

"Ooh." Michael pulls me closer to him, holds me tighter. I rock back and forth, clenching my stomach.

"Oooooh." I can't stop the moaning. It comes out between stuttering intakes of breath.

"Is Ryan a donor?" the male nurse asks in a break between my groans. "His vital organs are in no condition to donate of course, but you can donate his skin. And his bones. And you can donate his corneas."

I have to think about what he is saying. Dissect his words. It's all happening too fast. He is waiting for an answer, but I can't speak through my constricted throat, my runny nose, the flood of tears rolling down my face. I grab more tissues from the box on the table and press them to my eyes, my cheeks, my nose. Michael is silent. We both know this decision is mine to make.

The words sink in. Ryan's vital organs are so damaged that only his skin and his bones and his corneas are transplantable. A rush of imagery surfaces. How they might harvest skin and bone. My stomach threatens to erupt.

I focus on Ryan's Hershey-brown eyes. See them as clearly as if he were standing in front of me. The tenderness in them. Their sometimes-mischievous twinkle. "His corneas," I say, fighting to hold all the pieces of me together. "If they can go to a person. Not scientific research or anything like that."

"That can be done," the male nurse says. "We'll have the transplant team contact you."

CLOSURE

⚜

I have no idea how much time has passed. It's been distorted, taken out of its familiar framework. It might have been five minutes or an hour.

They ask if we want to see Ryan. We've been triple tag-teamed. Both nurses and the chaplain sit shoulder to shoulder to shoulder in chairs facing us. A wall of good intent that feels like a firing squad.

They seem to be shooting the same word bullets, one after another.

"You can see him if you want."

"You should see him."

"You need this for closure."

Not knowing who to direct my response to, I stare at the floor. "I don't know." My voice is thick. I'm terrified. Terrified of every decision and everything that will follow. Terrified to see my vibrant boy so badly damaged that I can't fix it. I've always fixed things for my children. Kissed their scrapes and stood them back on their feet again. That's what parents do.

"I'm afraid," I try to explain through the heaviness that has draped itself over me. "I'm afraid to see him suffering. In pain."

"He's not in pain," one of the women responds. I am not

sure if it is the female nurse or the chaplain. "You should see him for closure. You may regret it forever if you don't see him."

Moments pass as I consider this. *If I don't see him, will I regret it forever? Maybe.*

"Does he look hurt?" I ask.

"He doesn't look too bad." The male nurse again. "His nose and lower face are swollen, probably broken, but he has only one small facial laceration. And he has some incisions where tubes were placed to drain blood from his body cavity. But his body will be covered."

"Oh." Dissecting words again. "His face looks okay, then?"

"Yes. Swollen. His nose was broken. And that one small laceration on his forehead."

"Oh. I don't know."

I turn to Michael, the question written on my face. I note the answer written on his, then turn back to the trio.

"Maybe."

DESTINATION RYAN

Michael has tears running down his face and I can't stop the moaning as we follow behind the female nurse and the chaplain. Pat and Melissa trail behind us. No one objects. The nurse and chaplain lead us through a maze of corridors. The people we pass grow silent, stop to stare, somehow appending themselves to our personal tragedy.

They parade us into an elevator that goes up to who knows where. Destination: Ryan. The elevator comes to a halt, the doors open, the procession turns left and pauses after a short march down the hall.

"Here we are," someone says. "Right through this door."

I stop, shivering and frozen in place.

"I can't," I whisper. "I can't." The open doorway seems a barrier. Something I shouldn't breach. I know if I enter that room it will swallow me, and thrust me into a place of no return.

The others go in, come out. They urge me to see Ryan, assuring me he doesn't look too bad. Telling me I need this for closure. I might regret it forever if I don't. Their words hit me like a series of punches. Weaken me. So I step through the doorway even though I know I should avoid that room with all the force I can muster.

"Ryan?" The room is dim, and it takes my eyes a moment to adjust as I stand inside the door. Ryan is on a gurney, lying on his back, covered to his chin with a sheet. I search for the familiar, Ryan's face, and inch closer.

"Ryan?" Gray and swollen. There is blood pooled in his right ear and a drip, drip, dripping of something onto the floor from a part of his body I cannot see. An animal sound escapes me.

A part of me wants to lunge toward my son, gather him up in my arms, carry him from this room and say, *that's enough of this, we're going home now*. Instead, I continue my hesitant walk to the head of the gurney, drawn by Ryan's face. *Oh, Ryan.* His face is so terribly swollen.

When I do finally reach my boy, I turn to Michael and ask, "Is he cold?" I need to know before touching him. Michael nods his head, yes.

Ever so tenderly, I place my hands on either side of Ryan's head, afraid to touch his face for all the swelling. "Ryan?" I am desperate for him to answer me. A teardrop falls from my cheek onto his. Then another. A rainstorm, those audible drips onto the floor combined with these drops. As my tears roll down Ryan's face, I use my thumbs to wipe them away. "Don't cry, Ryan," I whisper. "Don't cry."

The others in the room stand silent, watching me. *Please let me be alone with him,* I beg, but the words stay lodged in my head. *Please leave me alone.*

I pledge in silence the words Ryan and I first exchanged when he was just three years old. *I love you how much big is the sky.* The words he still sometimes says to me in private, often in the abbreviated form. "How much big is the sky." The words I will never again hear him utter.

"I love you how much big is the sky, Ryan," I whisper. "I love you how much big is the sky." But he cannot hear me. I'm realizing that sometimes language dies with a single person.

Ryan, where are you?

Michael takes my arm. "Come on now," he urges but doesn't

demand. After only a moment of hesitation, I let Michael lead me out of the room.

I try not to think about what lies beneath the sheet. Or what should, but doesn't. I refuse to look again after that first unavoidable glance.

HOW MUCH BIG IS THE SKY

Ryan was suffering through another earache. He had them often as a young child, four or five times a year. It seemed they always flared in the middle of the night when his pediatrician wasn't available. It was one o'clock in the morning. Six-year-old Amber was sleeping in the other bedroom, and Ryan was in my bed whimpering. "It hurts mommy."

"I know honey. I'm sorry." His temperature was 101. I had given him a dose of children's liquid Tylenol and held a cool damp washcloth to his forehead. "I love you," I said. I wanted to hold him to me but feared making him even more uncomfortably hot, so instead I caressed his flushed cheek, brushed the damp sun-blond hair back from his face. And I sang to him, soft and slow. "Hush little baby, don't say a word, momma's gonna buy you a mocking bird." Then, "Swing lowwww, sweet charrrriot." Trying to relieve his pain with my touch and my song. Wishing him to sleep.

His eyes remained half-hooded.

"I love you," I said again.

"How big?" he asked.

He wasn't as flushed as he'd been when he stumbled into my bedroom just over an hour ago complaining that his ear hurt.

"Big," I said. "As big as can be."

I removed the washcloth from his forehead. The Tylenol was doing its work. He wasn't as hot now.

"How much big is the sky?" His voice was hushed, exhausted but persistent.

"Yes," I said. "I love you how much big is the sky," thinking those words are probably as good a way of conveying infinite love as any.

Ryan rolled over onto his side facing away from me and I covered him with the sheet. I switched off the light and climbed into bed with him, not too close, but close enough to smell him, his shampoo, his bath soap, his three-year-old boyness. Close enough to hear him mumble, "I love you how much big is the sky too."

THE SUN WILL RISE

The female nurse breaks the silence. "You have to make arrangements with a funeral director."

This immediately brings to mind our friend Bart, short for Barton, who works at a funeral home. Just as instantly I regret having once described his physical appearance—tall, thin, pale—as cadaverous. Not funny. *Forgive me.*

Evidently Bart is the first person who jumps to Michael's mind as well. He squeezes my hand and says, "Bart." I lower, then raise my chin.

The female nurse is the only one of the three hospital employees who remains with us. Pat, Melissa, Michael and me. I'm beginning to forgive her for going on and on about her son. She is providing needed guidance. We aren't well versed in the rituals of death.

I turn to her and ask in a voice too thick, "Now? Do we have to contact a funeral director now?" The words come slow, snarling their way through the grief that has settled.

"You need to do it soon," she says. "As soon as you get home."

This is it then. Ryan is no longer a patient. It's time to go.

Though the message is clear, I am terrified to face what comes next.

"So, I guess..."

The words don't come freely.

"I guess we should go then?"

The nurse nods her head and gets up from the chair she's been sitting in. Perhaps her shift is ending. Michael stands, looking down at me. Like reverse dominos, Pat gets up from his seat, and Melissa follows. As if our moves are choreographed, I stand on cue.

Michael turns to the nurse. "Thank you," he says as if she has just handed him a cupcake. She reaches for the door.

"Be careful on the ride home."

She turns the knob and the door opens to reveal a throng of teenagers in the hallway. Some I recognize as Ryan's friends and others I don't. They've been awfully quiet. I feel like I should say something. If I knew they were here, I might have thought of some words, but the surprise leaves me mute. Their faces are haunted, questioning, as they move up against one wall or the other to let us through. I can't meet their eyes, filled with expectation, so I focus on the floor and follow the heels of Michael's boots through the gauntlet. Pat follows me and Melissa follows him until Michael's heels come to a halt just outside of the hospital emergency department.

"We'll stop by later," Pat says, wrapping me in a bear hug. He releases me and his arms reach for Michael. Mine reach for Melissa. Pat and Melissa walk back into the hospital to join the other kids.

It surprises me that the sky is light now.

"The sun rose," I say as if there was a chance it wouldn't.

My head is foggy. Dense and numb. I'm operating on autopilot, controlled by the unknown. My own body conspires against me. My legs pull me forward as we walk to the car when what I want most, what I need, is to go backward. Retrace my steps back to yesterday.

"How do we tell Amber?" I ask Michael as he opens the passenger door. He responds by turning to face me. His eyes are glassy with tears, his lips set firm. I see from the tremble of his jaw that he can't speak. He shakes his head. I lift my right hand to his face and place my palm against his cheek. It's the only comfort I can offer. I leave it there several seconds, feeling his chin quiver, before sliding into the passenger seat.

On the drive to Amber's house, Michael sits straight behind the steering wheel, hands at ten o'clock and two, just as everyone in our generation was taught. He looks straight ahead at the road, revealing his patrician profile. He is either lost in thought or stunned silent.

The normal Saturday morning activity startles me. People rushing this way and that. A woman in a turquoise pea coat fills the gas tank of her bright yellow Chevy Blazer. A young man in the next lane sings to the beat of the music that vibrates the air outside his car. Two kids share a joke on the sidewalk.

I expected a more somber world.

How can it be that the sun rises at the same time that a son falls?

INFORMING AMBER

We are sitting in the Nissan staring at the cream-colored three-story Victorian. Neither of us is eager to take the next series of steps . . . open the car door, cross the sidewalk, follow the icy brick pathway, walk up the three stairs onto the porch, ring the doorbell, enter the house. Say the words I'm not so sure I believe. "Ryan is dead."

I'm dazed, like nothing is real. Like I am in some alternate universe that resembles the world I know, yet where everything is distorted.

I take a deep breath, exhale, and reach for the door handle. I don't know what I will say, but I know I have to be the one to say it. How do you tell your daughter that her little brother is dead? Her only sibling? Amber, who will apologize to a plant for snipping a dying leaf. Who will remove the leaf from the room so the plant won't see its severed limb.

"Ready?" Michael asks.

"I'll never be ready for this," I say, opening the car door. Michael joins me at the curb. We stand in the morning chill looking at the house for a moment longer. It is nestled between two other homes of similar size and appearance, half-way up the hill that leads to the upper crossroad. Michael touches the small of my back, prompting me forward.

"Maybe it doesn't work," Michael says, pushing the doorbell a second time. He may be right. I don't hear a chime.

Just then the sound of the deadbolt being unlocked reaches us, and the door opens. Amber's waist-length chestnut hair, still blond-streaked by the summer sun, is untamed. We must have woken her. She's wearing one of her long Indian-print dresses. My little hippie.

"What's wrong?" she asks.

"Amber," I choke. I'm not sure I can even talk now.

"What?" She swings the heavy wooden door open wider so we can enter. Closes it behind us. Searches my eyes, then Michael's.

"It's Ryan. He was in a car crash." The fright contorts her face.

"Is he okay?"

"No." I reach out to hug her to me.

She is beginning to comprehend what I'm trying to tell her, but I owe it to her to be as clear as possible. "He . . . he couldn't survive."

"Oooooh," her voice is long and pining. She pulls from me and holds her stomach, looking up at me—confusion, shock, and grief merging on her face.

"Nooo." I wrap my arms around her again. I hear my own words of resistance come from deep within her, over and over. I didn't know until now that so much of the language of grief is spoken through elongated "ohs" and "nos."

"But how . . ." Amber starts. She pushes away again to probe my eyes. Her face is a frozen cry. Confusion furrows her brow.

"We don't know. Come home with us."

Amber shakes her head. "Mike and Kalum are still asleep," she says. "I should let them sleep."

I glance at the clock on the wall. Not quite eight in the morning.

Amber drops to the floor, puts her elbows on her crossed legs and holds her head in her hands.

"But I'm worried about your being alone," I insist. "Shouldn't you wake up Mike?"

"I *need* to be alone right now," Amber says, and I understand. I need some time alone with this too. So I can stop being brave. So I can figure out how to fix it.

"We'll stop by later," Amber promises.

O CHRISTMAS TREE

The first thing I see when we get home is the decorated Christmas tree.

"We shouldn't have put the tree up," I tell Michael. There is too much cheer in the room. The dogs with their excitement and wagging tails. The tree, standing there at center stage, exuding all of its optimism. The star on top, brushing the ceiling. The full branches laden with ornaments—family heirlooms, kid crafts, Victorian garnishes—and strung with colored mini lights. I close my eyes and turn my head, but not before making note of the wrapped presents under the tree. *What are we going to do with Ryan's Christmas presents now?* I try to turn my mind off.

"We need to make the arrangements," Michael says. "Do you think it's too early to call Bart?"

God, I can't handle this. I turn from Michael and tread up the stairs, clutching the rail, hefting one leaden foot after another. At the top of the stairway, I take a right, avoiding a glance to the left at Ryan's room. I trudge through the master bedroom into the bathroom, close the door, sink to the floor, and hug my knees to my chest. I hear myself groan, low and guttural like an animal, long and hard, again and again and again.

Michael's footsteps sound like a warning as they make their

way up the steps, through our bedroom, down the hall leading to the master bath. Getting closer, louder now. I suppress the moaning as best I can. It comes out as soft whines.

"Sher?"

I just want to be left alone. I can't make any decisions right now. Maybe he'll go away.

"Can we meet with the funeral director this morning?" Michael asks through the bathroom door.

My voice takes a minute to find itself. "This morning?" Stuffy sounding, reaching him through the sludge of emotion. Everything is happening too fast.

"He says it's best. To have as much flexibility as possible for scheduling," Michael says. "You never know what might happen." My mind does the translation: someone else might die and take the date and time we would prefer.

MAKING ARRANGEMENTS

I know how you feel," the funeral director says. "I have a nineteen-year-old son myself."

Oh no, not this again. Please don't, I beg in silence as he proceeds to tell us about his son. I try to drown him out with the words in my head, *please don't, please*—sitting trapped and still.

"I can't imagine—" he begins.

"Neither can I," I say. "Neither can I." The words come out soft but I feel the power of them. They stop him in mid-sentence.

The funeral director asks questions. I stare at his shoes.

Black and polished. Shiny.

"Do you know where he will be interred?"

"Ryan? No, not yet."

"What date were you thinking of for the funeral?"

I raise my head to Michael as he turns to look at me. Shake my head. "We don't know."

Leather, I decide. His shoes are definitely leather.

The funeral director summarizes the various services they offer. All I hear are words like interment, funeral, embalmed, wake, obituary, cemetery, casket. A foreign language. I never realized before now that death has its own language.

"We have a variety of casket to choose from. Bart can show you. Do you know what kind of casket you would like?" I look at Bart, sitting to the right of the funeral director, dressed in a dark suit. Familiar, yet unfamiliar. I am used to seeing him on the volleyball court, or at informal gatherings. I never expected to be sitting with him like this. As a client.

Bart leads us to a coffin showroom. I am surprised there is such a thing, yet here we are in a room with all these many different styles of coffins. Like a car dealer, only these are caskets. There is a pink one and a blue one, and lots of various shades of wooden ones, the most ornate sitting in positions of prominence. I turn to Michael, "What kind of coffin do you think Ryan would like?" My own words sound ludicrous to me.

I am drawn to the blue one, thinking back to the bright fall day that someone asked Ryan what his favorite color was. I try to remember who asked him the question. I can't. But I do remember being surprised at the sophistication of Ryan's answer. He said, "It depends on what it is," and gave an example. "The blue of the sky today, that's my favorite color of blue for the sky."

The color of the casket reminds me of the blue of the sky that day. But that might not be Ryan's favorite color for a casket. And it's one of the cheaper ones. We both know Ryan wouldn't like cheap, so we choose a nice shiny oak casket with brass handles.

That decision made, Bart leads us to the vaults.

"Why do we need a vault?" I ask him.

"To protect the casket and—everything—from the elements."

"But why?" I want to know. Michael puts his hand on my shoulder and chooses a vault.

We walk back into the consultation room to rejoin the

funeral director and sit down in the same chairs we sat in when we first arrived. Like assigned seating.

Italian leather, I think, reestablishing my focus on the funeral director's shoes. They have little breathing holes on the top. Over his toes.

"He will probably have an autopsy," the funeral director says. "We'll have to take that into consideration."

"An autopsy?" My head snaps up and I search his face. Pasty. Dark hair. Well-manicured.

"An autopsy?"

"Probably. We'll coordinate everything."

"I don't want Ryan to have an autopsy."

"Well . . ." he says. "When they die that way."

"But I don't want him to have an autopsy," I say, more forceful now.

He taps his right foot to fill the silence, the foot that will reunite him with that nineteen-year-old son he has himself. That living, breathing nineteen-year-old son.

"I don't want Ryan to have an autopsy," I say again, more to myself than to anyone within hearing distance.

It's clear to me now that I've been stripped of all authority and control.

The pointy toe goes up and down.

The thin black laces keep rhythm, as if to music.

WANDERING

Michael makes the phone calls and the news travels fast. People stop by bringing with them food and condolences. First Robbie, another of Ryan's best friends, and Robbie's mother Lois. And then there is a steady flow.

I can't manage people yet. I wander the house lost, looking for Ryan. Evidence of Ryan. I stare at photos, walk into Ryan's bedroom, lie on his bed and breathe him in. I look out the window for Ryan's truck, listen for the sound of it coming up the drive, wait for him to burst through the door. I cross paths with Ryan's dog, Nova, who knows in her quiet intuitive manner that something is wrong with her boy. She gets in my way and I get in hers. I give her an understanding pat. She licks my hand. She lies on Ryan's bed. She sits waiting at the door. We gaze into each other's eyes and see ourselves.

Ryan, where are you? We need you home now. Please come home.

Amber, Mike, and Kalum were at the house when we returned from meeting with the funeral director. Between the wandering and the condolence activity, we all sit in the living room and try to act normal for Kalum. I avert my eyes each time they threaten to rest on the unlit Christmas tree. Whenever the tree does come into my line of vision, I glare at it. I want to take it down. But Michael says we should keep it up so Kalum can have a Christmas.

"It's a good thing we took that photograph," Amber says, referring to the picture I insisted on following Thanksgiving dinner. It's a photo of Ryan, Amber, Kalum, and Michael. I'm not in it. I'm usually on the other side of the camera.

"I know," I say, doing the math. "Just nine days ago," I add, thankful, but with regret so massive it lodges in my throat. Wishing I had taken more. *You didn't know*, I try to pardon myself, but it doesn't work. I push off the love seat and head upstairs.

Ryan's bedroom door is ajar. Nova is on his bed again, lying on her side. She turns her head slightly to the right at my approach and raises her eyes to meet mine. Even as I enter Ryan's room, I wonder if I should let her be, go the opposite direction into my own bedroom. But she looks so forlorn.

"Hey Nova girl," I manage. "Good girl." I smooth her head, then cup my right hand under her snout, pet her neck with the other. Trying to comfort her.

Her bulk takes up most of the bed. I plop down and fit myself between the wall and the dog, molding around Nova's spine, right arm sprawled over her shoulders. Bury my face in her folds.

"I know, Nova." She lays her face on my hand. "I know."

PUPPIES

Nova and her sister Nanauk came into our lives almost seven years ago. It had been a difficult year. Losing Spirit, the dog the kids grew up with, to a relationship ended. A move from one town to another. From one school to another. All the adjustments young teenagers have to make as a result. Leaving old friends, trying to fit in with the new. So when the German Shepard down the road had pups and the kids asked me if they could each have one, I said yes. Every day they visited those puppies.

Amber did her homework. She interviewed the owner. The pups were a mix of Shepard, Doberman, and Retriever. They would grow to be big dogs. She researched each of the breeds, determined their average life span, identified diseases they might be prone to. "Is there a family history of hip dysplasia?" Amber asked the disinterested owner. He threw his head back and snorted. He was just trying to get rid of the mutts that were pooping all over his back deck.

There were a dozen pups in the litter. After close evaluation Amber and Ryan each chose one. Amber selected the solitary puppy that seemed to be shunned by her siblings and named her Nanauk. A fitting name for a family pet. Ryan chose the runt of the litter and named her Nova. I initially thought Ryan named Nova after an astronomical term—the brightest star. I basked in the brilliance of it. But no.

"I named her after Nathan's Chevy," Ryan said.

I tried to dissuade Ryan from choosing the tiny barrel-chested pup, the weakest of them all. Her health worried me. But Ryan had fallen in love while waiting for Nova to mature for adoption and there was no talking him out of it.

A rainstorm on a bitter-cold April evening brought the pups home. The litter had been left unprotected on the outside deck. A neighbor alerted us, and we went on a rescue mission. A week before the official adoption date, Nova and Nanauk were welcomed into our family.

BEAUTY SCAR OR PROOF IS IN THE EVIDENCE

"What happened?" we ask the kids who drop by. We have so many questions and we haven't yet heard from the police. Michael called the state barracks and asked to talk to the officer in charge of the investigation, but he was no longer on duty.

"He'll be in on Monday," the dispatcher said. "You can leave a message or call back then."

I already know weekends are a tough time to be born. If there are problems. If you need certain tests, they have to wait for Monday. Now I'm learning weekends are a tough time to die. Even as you make arrangements to bury your son. If you need certain answers, they have to wait for Monday. Ryan's life, sandwiched between these two weekends.

Despite the obstacles, snippets of information filter to us.

"How did you get into the Family Room at the hospital?" I ask Pat and Melissa.

"I told them Ryan was my brother," Pat says.

"And I said I was his girlfriend," Melissa adds.

"Was Ryan driving?" I direct my question to Pat.

"No."

"Who was he with?"

"Kellie and Dave," Pat says.

"Dave who?" I ask, surprised that I am reminded of the old Cheech and Chong comedy skit.

Pat gives me a last name.

I search my memory but I can't place him.

"Are they okay?"

"Yeah, they'll be okay."

"Good," I say through a blanket of relief that confuses me. I didn't know grief and relief were compatible, but here they are sitting side-by-side. "Who was driving?"

Pat looks away for a second, and then after making some silent decision turns back to me. "Dave," he says.

Whatever sugar-coated curtain of protection that was shielding me is stripped away with the realization that this kid is alive and Ryan is not.

I turn away and head back to the cocoon of my bedroom. It takes some time because I am suddenly very, very heavy.

∽

I FIND myself in the full-length bedroom mirror. Ryan's brown Enyce shirt, the one he wore in that last photograph, drapes me from shoulder to thigh. The long sleeves bunch at my wrists. I raise the front of the shirt and cup it with my hands to my nose and mouth. Smell it. Take in Ryan's scent. Old Spice and fresh air. Tucking the shirt up under my chin, I unbutton my jeans, drop the waistline three inches, and stare at the Beauty Scar that stretches across my lower abdomen—that violent eight inches of a gash centered between my hips. I've always called it my Beauty Scar and I've worn it with pride, the emergency escape route that safely delivered my baby boy into the world.

Proof of Ryan's life.

Now evidence. Evidence that Ryan once lived.

It's a new thought I try to purge, but some thoughts are persistent.

My expression contorts in the mirror and I see *The Scream* captured on my face. The anguish I never understood in the painting by Edvard Munch stares back at me, and I understand it now. I sink to my hands and knees and then fold myself into a fetal position on the floor. I cover my mouth with my left hand and press the palm of my right hand against my Beauty Scar.

"I can't do this Ryan." I stifle *The Scream* coming from my own throat by pressing harder on my mouth. "I can't live without you. I can't do it." Only when I realize I am biting my hand and smashing my forehead against the bookcase, do I stop myself.

THE LAST SUPPER

Sometimes it's the laughter that haunts.

The day before the crash, Michael called me at work and told me he was going grocery shopping. Did I want anything special or in particular?

"How about lobster for dinner?" I asked him. It was Friday, and I didn't expect to be home much later than six-thirty that evening. The past few weeks were filled with celebration. Michael's birthday in late October, then Halloween, then the birthday Ryan and I shared on November 18, then Thanksgiving. Now it was December 6. Christmas was right around the corner. The tree was up and decorated, wrapped presents beneath it. It felt like a fine time to celebrate with a lobster dinner.

A while later Amber called me. "Where are you?" I asked.

"Your house," she answered.

I heard excited laughter in the background. Then, "Kaaaylum!" Ryan's voice carried through the phone.

"What's going on?"

"Ryan and Kalum are shoveling the walkway," Amber said. The storm the night before had dropped a good foot of snow.

We both were silent for a moment, listening to "the boys," as

I called them. I heard Ryan shout another long, "Kaaay-lum," followed by a muffled splat and Kalum's not-quite-three-years-young raucous giggle.

"Well, they sound like they're having a great time doing it," I chuckled.

"Yeah. More play than work. They're throwing snowballs now."

We both listened to them for a moment longer, me through the phone line. Amber may have been watching through the window. It put a smile on my face. Ryan and Kalum were so close.

"Are you staying for dinner?" I asked Amber, thinking that if she was, I'd better call Michael and have him pick up another lobster for Kalum and something different for Amber, who won't eat lobster.

"No, I have to go home soon," Amber replied.

Michael called me again later in the afternoon. "When do you think you might be leaving?" he asked.

"I'm not sure now," I told him. "Probably late." I was helping to manage a complex integration project involving the company's most recent acquisition. "I'm sorry," I added.

"Well, Ryan's hungry," Michael said. "Should I let him have his lobster now, or would you rather he wait?"

"Go ahead and let him eat now if he's hungry," I said. So Ryan ate his lobster.

Afterward, Michael recalls overhearing a phone call Ryan received. Someone was trying to convince him to go out. Michael remembers Ryan saying, no, he didn't want to go out. He was tired. But whoever called was persistent. Eventually, someone convinced him to go out. He left the house after eating his lobster before I got home from work.

Later that evening I said to Michael, "I wonder where Ryan is. Do you think I should call him?"

Then the justification that swayed me against it. *It's not that late. He's nineteen now.* The memory of the embarrassment we caused a few months earlier when he hadn't answered his phone. Calling all his friends, driving around going door to door after midnight, finding him asleep at a buddy's house.

"You worry too much mom," Ryan had said.

PHOTOGRAPHS AND MEMORIES

Amber, Melissa and I are on the floor in the center of the living room working on a photo collage for the wake. We're using poster board that Billy's family gave to Melissa for Ryan. The extra poster board leftover from Billy's wake less than three months ago.

"Remember this kid, mom?" Ryan had asked when he brought Billy to the house last summer.

"Billy!" I felt buried in his hug. "My goodness, you've grown." Ryan and Billy were inseparable in middle school but lost touch when we moved to the next town over. He was still the Billy I remembered, but twice the size.

It was right around that time when Ryan announced at the dinner table he was thinking of buying a motorcycle.

"Ryan, please don't do that," I said. "I'd live in constant fear if you had a motorcycle." He let me talk him out of it, but not before informing me that he was eighteen now and old enough to make his own decisions.

Less than three months later, Billy died in a motorcycle crash. Ryan was stunned by it. I cried with abandon at the funeral.

"I wouldn't be able to survive if anything like this happened to you or Amber or Kalum," I told Ryan following Billy's funeral. "Thank you so much for not getting a motorcycle." I wrapped my arms around him and said, "I love you how much big is the sky."

That was the last time Ryan heard those words from me. Right after Billy's funeral. Two months before Ryan's nineteenth birthday. Just short of three months ago. And now we are using the poster board from Billy's wake for Ryan's.

"Oh, God," I say aloud, verbal fallout from memories that are more than I can bear. Both Amber and Melissa look up.

"It's unbelievable," I try to explain. "Isn't it unbelievable?" I wish I could have captured Ryan and Billy in a bubble that summer day and carried them into the future beyond the dates that took their lives. Brought them safely to today. I wish . . .

There is a tap at the front door. Michael opens it and my mother steps into the entrance hall.

"Hi, June." Michael gives her a hug.

"Hi, mom." The words come out in a sigh as I push myself off the floor to greet her. She walks forward into the living room and onto the poster board, stepping on a photo of Ryan's smiling face. Like the momentum that propelled her from Maryland to Connecticut for the services has a mind of its own and isn't quite ready to stop. Amber and Melissa gasp.

"Oh, I'm sorry." She steps back revealing the edges of the damaged photo cupping the depression left by her damp boot print. Everyone in the room is silent, staring at the marred photo. The most precious things in the world right now are the photographs.

Unbelievable.

CEMETERY

I didn't even know this cemetery was here," I tell the elderly sexton. The wind grabs the plot map he holds in his hands and threatens to run off with it. Michael steps forward to catch the loose side. Even standing in the protection offered by the sexton's old station wagon with its rear liftgate up, the wind whips at us. My eyes water. Ears sting. Amber is standing opposite me, hunched over with her back to the wind, the hood of her thick winter jacket protecting her head, hands buried deep in the pockets.

Barren is the word that comes to mind as I evaluate the area. Small. We turned left from Main Street onto the road with no name that ends at the sewage plant. Then right, through the stone pillars into Coventry Cemetery, hidden behind the Catholic cemetery in town whose name everyone knows. I don't like it.

"But it's close," I say aloud, almost as a rebuttal to myself. "What, about three miles from home?" I glance at Michael, then Amber. Neither of them answers. "That's important," I add, knowing I will be spending a lot of time at the cemetery. "Close is very important."

"It is close," Michael says. The tip of his nose is red.

Looking at the foot or so of snow covering the ground, I realize we will need easy access to Ryan. Otherwise, I'd be out here with a snow shovel digging a path.

"Do you have anything right off the cemetery drive?"

"Well . . ."

Helped by Michael, the sexton lays the plot map in the back of the station wagon. The map wears its history in the form of wrinkles and stains and tears.

"We have these available here." The sexton runs an aged finger along the map. "And these." Some lots have surnames on them. Others are blank.

"Do you want a single grave?"

"No," I respond, even though we haven't discussed it as a family. A single grave sounds too lonely.

I assess the cemetery again. The squared fieldstone columns standing at the entrance give it some character. And just beyond, directly across the unnamed road is an open field bordering the river. I can see the potential.

"We want four together. Do you have four together right off the drive?"

"Are you going to want an upright monument?" the sexton asks. "Or a flat marker?" Another thing we hadn't discussed.

Gazing around, I see that none of the flat markers are visible. They are all covered with snow. "He'll want a monument." I'm making decisions on the fly. Neither Amber nor Michael intervenes.

"Well, you want two double lots then. There's this. And this." The sexton points to our options with a yellow crusted fingernail.

It is clear to me which of the available lots are most desirable.

"We'll take these," I gesture. "Closer to the flagpole. Ryan is very patriotic."

THE CROSS

"Mom," Amber shouts from downstairs. She and Kalum are almost always at the house now. "Pat's here."

It takes all my strength to respond, lift my head from the pillow, roll over, bring myself to a sitting position, place my feet on the floor, stand up.

"Okay," I manage, but not loud enough to be heard. Or maybe I didn't say it at all.

Amber stomps up the stairs and pauses outside the closed bedroom door, offers a quick knock. "Pat's here," she says. "He wants to talk to you."

"Okay," I say with more force.

One step, I urge myself. *One moment at a time.* And that's how I make it to the bedroom door, to the hallway.

I peer down at Pat from the top of the stairs. He is standing in the front entry bearing a three-foot-tall, white-washed wooden cross. "We made it," he says, pride in his voice. The shadows and movements of other kids on the porch outside the front door behind him suggest a crowd.

"The lady who owns the house doesn't mind if we put it up," he assures me. "I already talked to her."

My comprehension is slow to kick in, so I say nothing, examining the homemade structure in his arms.

The Cross has writing on it. Words of love and farewell expressed in many different hands. Pat digs into the pocket of his ski jacket, pulls out a black marker, and hands it up in my direction. Now I get it. The center of The Cross has been left blank, a place of prominence for Ryan's family. I shake my head, no. Pat prods the marker toward me again.

"No," I say, oddly touched. "I can't."

How can I tell Pat that I can't write any words of farewell? That I'm still bargaining with God? That I'm not so sure Ryan won't come back?

He urges, I resist. Amber writes something. Michael writes something. Amber leaves with the kids to place The Cross at the accident scene.

I turn toward the haven of my bedroom, giving silent apology to all those families whose crosses I have passed in my lifetime. Now I understand what it means.

A grieving mom appreciates every little memorial. Even a lonely cross set on the shoulder of a deadly curve at the side of a country road.

PREPARING FOR THE WAKE

༄

"What about a veil?" I ask the funeral director. When he doesn't answer I persist. "Where can I get a mourning veil?" To fill the silence, I add, "To hide my face."

I notice the softness in his eyes and recognize it as compassion.

"Women don't wear mourning veils anymore," he says.

"Oh." Never one for public display, I'm wondering how I will hide my face then.

"Are you ready to see him?" he asks, drawing us back to the matter at hand.

"Ryan?" Amber, Michael, and I assess one another.

I touch Amber's arm. "Ready?" I ask, worried about how she will survive this. Her baby brother. Her only sibling. The one who shared her childhood history.

"I think so," she says.

The undertaker leads us into a large adjoining room in the old brick funeral home. The casket is near the far wall and it takes us several hesitant steps to get close enough to see inside.

The top half of the casket is open, exposing Ryan to his waist. His face doesn't look like Ryan's face. It is so swollen and ghastly pale. That pencil-point thin strip of hair tracing his once chiseled jaw is uneven. *He wouldn't like that*, I think, just before realizing his hair must still be growing for his shave line to be rough and crooked like that. My body stiffens. I forget to breathe.

Oh, God, parts of Ryan are still living. I don't say it aloud because it adds to the horror somehow. I hope Amber doesn't notice and steal a glance at her. She is staring at her brother with silent tears streaking down her face. I take her hand and turn back to Ryan.

"How does he look?" the funeral director asks.

What a bizarre question. I stumble for an answer. Truth be told he looks awful. Nearly unrecognizable. Like he was terribly hurt before he died. Not good at all.

Amber and Michael stare at the floor. I shut my eyes tight and bow my own head. *Oh. God Ryan. I am so sorry.* I'm sorry that I can't fix this, that I didn't prevent it. I'm sorry that I don't know what to do. A whine escapes from my throat.

The tap of the funeral director's shoe lifts my chin. Another tap turns my eyes to meet his.

With a level of control that surprises me, I hear myself ask, "Can you tidy up his shave line? Ryan was very precise about that."

THE WAKE

The best of Ryan's friends linger after the wake. They were the first to arrive over four hours ago and now they are reluctant to leave.

"Do you mind if I give Ryan my gold chain?" Pat asks.

"Of course not." My heart is full of gratitude and love for these kids.

Amber helps Pat lift Ryan's head. Rusty fluid spills from the right side of Ryan's mouth. Pat and Amber freeze for a moment. I catch the fluid with a tear-dampened tissue before it drips onto the satin-white pillow in the casket, amazed at how well Amber is carrying herself. They manage to get Pat's gold neck chain in place. Colby and CC step closer and leave their gold neck chains with Ryan as well. Pat places a baseball cap on Ryan's head, then raises his eyes at me as if to ask if it's okay. I nod. A girl whose name I don't remember places a sachet of roses in his coffin.

Earlier, hundreds of people stood waiting in the December chill. The procession extended outside the funeral home, wrapped around the building, down the street, and circled the block. They streamed into the funeral home through a side entry and snaked through a maze of rooms and doorways. They paused at the photo collages, gazed at Ryan's Tae Kwon Do trophies, and one after another held out a hand to brush his snowboard. Most were crying when they reached us. Their embraces felt like they were clinging to their own dear lives.

They offered condolences. *I am so sorry for your loss . . . you are in my thoughts and prayers . . . there are no words . . . trust that God had another plan for him . . . this too shall pass . . . he is in a better place . . . Ryan was a great kid—you should be proud . . . God doesn't give a person more than they can bear . . . only the good die young . . . time will heal. . . you are so strong . . . God took him for a reason . . . I don't know how you are handling this so well.*

Some words comforted. Some words hurt. Some words elicited quiet anger and self-admonition to let it go.

Now Amber is addressing the kids who have stayed. She says things to them I should say, such as how special they each are to Ryan, how honored he would be that they are here. I am so proud of my first-born child. She is operating on sheer determination, all the while falling apart with heartbreak.

Then it is done. As reluctant as the truest of Ryan's friends are to leave, the restless shadows in the background convey to us that the inevitable time has come. The shadow movement gets closer and then the funeral director and someone else is at our side. The kids give us hugs before they filter out.

"What do you want to do with these things?" The funeral director asks as he gestures to the inside of the casket.

"We want them to stay with him."

"Everything?"

"Yes, everything."

"Even this?" he asks pointing to the small sachet of roses. The petite young girl who placed them there is gone now. She had sobbed and sobbed the whole time she was here.

"Yes," I said, "even that. Everything."

MICHAEL

*J*ust over a year after we welcomed Nova and Nanauk into our family, Michael and I met on a beach volleyball court.

The kids and I were living on Lake Wangumbaug in Coventry. Our summer water toys were a WaveRunner and a paddleboat. Ryan and the neighborhood boys fished off our dock. Amber avoided them when they were fishing because she can't stand to see a hook in the mouth of a fish. The kids and the dogs lived in the water.

I saw a volleyball game in progress on Lisicke Beach as I cruised by on the WaveRunner one summer evening. Maybe I learned the games were open to residents from a town newsletter. I don't remember. But I wanted to play, so I enlisted my friend Kirsten to join me and we showed up unannounced the following week.

Most of the players were about my age. A few of them were much younger or older. Michael welcomed us, explained the rules. He was in charge.

I was a novice, just looking for some exercise and fun. The kids were teenagers now, more independent. I had some time to explore my interests.

We all bonded on the volleyball court that summer. My game improved. A group of us began to spend time together off the court. We met each other's families. It was a good mix of personalities. Our intellects and senses of humor meshed.

The seeds of more than one marriage took root that summer on the beach volleyball court.

THE FUNERAL

*A*s the limousine turns from the highway exit ramp onto Main Street in Manchester we are greeted by the incredible stone architecture of the Methodist church looming ahead. The massive slate roof, the aged copper trimmings.

"Our church," Michael and I call it, having attended the mandatory counseling and Sunday services leading up to our wedding two-and-a-half years ago. A step toward religion but not a plunge. We chose this church for the beauty of its design.

I experience none of the awe the sight normally brings. The churning in my stomach grows more pronounced the closer we get. As the chauffeur parks the limousine. As we walk up the granite steps. As we enter the church through the oversized wooden doors garnished with thick, wrought-iron hardware.

A church official is waiting. He ushers Michael and me, followed by Amber, Kalum, and Mike into an open alcove to the left of the central entrance. We are to wait here while people enter the church for the funeral. He rushes off before I realize how uncomfortable I am sitting here exposed like this. But the man doesn't return, and when we do see him again, he is opening the immense front doors to let the streams of people in.

People who cannot help but stare at us, then away, and whisper to one another. I want to hide.

"Why did they put us here?" I lean into Michael. "Visible like this?" I wish there was a door to close.

"I don't know," Michael says, tired, resigned. "We're supposed to walk in after everyone's seated."

Kalum fusses. Mike picks him up and paces.

"I don't like this house daddy," Kalum says.

"Shhh," Mike says.

"I wish we could be seated now," I press, thinking they never should have done away with that mourning veil. I don't want anyone to see me, my face, my tears. There are so many people. I close my eyes and rest my head on Michael's shoulder. We sit and wait without speaking while people stream in to find a seat in the nave of the church.

After the crowd thins, we watch the undertaker's assistants roll the casket into the vestibule and the man who sat us here returns to gather us into place. Music commences.

The man positions me and Michael side-by-side behind the casket. Amber and Mike, with Kalum in his arms, stand behind us. I wonder where my mother is.

The casket leads us down the center aisle toward the altar and our seats at the front of the church. Michael holds my arm just as Ryan did on our wedding day when he escorted me to my husband-to-be, his stepfather-to-be. Ryan's smile exuding pride and all the confidence the promise of a bright future will bring.

But Ryan is in a coffin now, and this time I don't want to walk down that aisle. The fear that's been clinging to my insides since The Phone Call clutches harder. I can more easily drop to the floor than keep walking toward that altar. I stumble and Michael tightens his grip on my arm. I want to turn around and run out of this place as fast as I can, backward in time to where Ryan is still alive.

My eyes fixate on the closed casket. It occurs to me that I will never see Ryan again. Ever.

"Wait," I tug Michael's arm. "I need to see him again."

"Sher," he warns.

I lean into him. "No one told me I couldn't see him again."

I'm hyperventilating, gasping for breath now.

Michael puts an arm around my back to buoy me up and propel me forward.

"No. I can't—"

"For Ryan," he whispers in my ear. Words that give me just enough strength to continue placing one black high-heeled shoe in front of the other.

They leave the casket at the altar. The church official directs us to sit in the first row on the bench to the right. Mike, still holding Kalum, scoots in, followed by Amber, then me, then Michael. The long length of the bench behind us is empty, probably designated for immediate family members. Again, I wonder where my mother is.

The pastor begins. "We are met in this solemn moment to commend Ryan into the hands of Almighty God, our heavenly Father. In the presence of death, Christians have sure ground for hope and confidence and even for joy . . ." *Hope and joy?* ". . . because the Lord Jesus Christ, who shared our human life and death, was raised again triumphant and lives forevermore . . ." *Hope and joy?*

We stand up and sit down. Psalm 130, a hymn, the Lord's Prayer. My uncle Donald chokes through a poem I wrote, "How Will I Learn to Live Without You?" Some of Ryan's friends speak. I wish the pastor hadn't limited the number of speakers. I am desperate to hear their words. Desperate for everyone to hear their words.

"I want to go to Nana and Grandpa's house," Kalum says. He repeats this over and over until his father carries him out.

We sing. "A-a-maaa-zing grace, how sweet the sound . . ." and I hear the tap-tapping footsteps of someone walking toward us down the main passageway. There is some rustling before the footsteps rest somewhere behind us. Though I do not turn around to look, I know it is my mother come too late.

    I silently apologize to Ryan on her behalf. I worry he can somehow see this. Through the remaining minutes of the funeral service, I urge him not to be bothered by it. *It is nothing,* I tell him. *Don't you think a thing of it. Focus on all the other hundreds of people here who love you.*

    At the end, teenage pallbearers carefully raise the casket. Ryan's cousin and friends shoulder the weight of him as Ryan leads us away from the alter to some inconceivable future.

    The church bell wails out from deep within its hollow. *Don't. Go. Don't. Go. Don't. Go.* It doesn't restrain its cries, bellowing the words that echo in my head. *Don't go, Ryan.*

PROCESSION

"Wow," Amber says, awe in her voice. "Look." She's staring out of the rear window of the limousine we are in, which is following the hearse to the cemetery two towns away. We turn to follow her gaze. The funeral procession behind us seems to have no end. We must be a mile down the highway, yet in the far distance we can see the uninterrupted line of headlights still streaming onto Route 384 from the entrance ramp.

See Ryan? All these people are here for you. I feel a strange sense of pride that doesn't fit well with the other emotions that have invaded my body.

Mike took Kalum to our house after they left the church, so it's just Amber, Michael and me in the limo. We sit mostly silent during the ride, our ability to communicate the way we used to has been quashed, the lightness and humor gone. I stare at the back window of the hearse in front of us. It leads us down the highway, onto Route 44, through the town of Bolton, into Coventry. I'm worried the cemetery is too small to accommodate all the vehicles. The line of cars behind us is longer than the eye can see. As we drive down Main Street through our hometown, we pass the kids' former elementary school. There is a police car guarding the entrance to Coventry's Lisicke Beach. A law enforcement officer stands outside the cruiser in the gray chill watching the funeral procession pass. The lake is not yet frozen. It sits abandoned in the season that lurks between summer boating and winter skating.

"They plowed it," Michael says. "Good."

"That's nice," I respond, meaning not only is it nice that the town plowed the snow from the parking area, but also nice that they are letting us use the lot for any overflow parking needed for the reception at our house. Nice that the officer is guarding the entrance.

"Do you think there's enough space though?"

"I don't know," Michael says.

The hearse escorts us past the private road leading to our home, the middle school the kids attended, the fire station and town hall. I dig my heels into the floor mat, trying to stop the forward momentum. I don't want to go any farther. Like a tug-of-war, the hearse is winning. It pulls us past the post office, the corner store, the antique shop, the library. All the places familiar to Ryan. All the places he won't be entering or passing again. Then the hearse turns left, directed by another police officer onto the short stretch of the unnamed road leading to Coventry Cemetery.

ASHES TO ASHES

The hearse takes the long way to Ryan's grave to allow the greatest number of cars into the cemetery. Someone plowed the field across the road for overflow parking. They must have received permission from the landowner to use it. The gratitude and whatever relief I can muster comes out with a sigh. Everything has to be flawless for Ryan. I try not to let myself dwell on the things that were less than perfect. Like the fact that they couldn't get Ryan's music to play at the wake. That the pastor had us cut the list of speakers in half. That . . .

"Hush," I tell the beasts in my mind. "Shhh."

The limousine stops a car-length behind the hearse. The area surrounding Ryan's grave has been shoveled out. There is a rectangle of fake grass on the ground. All I can think of is the hole beneath it. My nose begins to burn and I feel the tears on my face. I want to rage against the world, but instead my head drops, my shoulders bow and I fall into myself. Michael touches my arm as the limousine driver opens his side door to let us out.

"It's cold," I say as the wind whips in. I cannot help but think the wind is Ryan's last rebellious act. He did not want to die young. He was forward-thinking. He had plans. I close my eyes trying to extinguish the thoughts. I can't suppress the long groan as I expel all the breath in my body, test how it feels not to breathe again. It's easy, this not breathing. I want to fall into oblivion, but the words Michael spoke earlier come back to me. *For Ryan*, he said. I lift my head and take a breath, hold tight to Michael's hand as I step from the limousine.

The cemetery is full now. Someone directs cars to park in the plowed field. Cold slush seeps into the pointed toes of my high heels. The bottom of my skirt whips at my calves in the wind. My hair flogs my face. I have a strange vision of myself from above. The lady draped in black. The elements beating her down. *Numb me*, I beseech the wind.

"Ryan's music," I say to Michael. I can't talk in full sentences anymore. Michael places his hand on the shoulder of the limo driver and whispers something in his ear. The chauffeur scurries off.

The shivering huddle grows denser as people make their way from their vehicles. Amber is weeping. I sidle up to her and drape my arm around her waist. Ryan's music mix begins to play, and the crowd continues to expand as Sarah McLachlan sings, "I Will Remember You." The shoveled area around the grave isn't large enough. Some people are standing up to their knees in snow.

As we continue to wait for everyone to gather, Linkin Park croons the lyrics of "My December." The crowd is silent, listening to the music.

Chris walks up. "Can I read the poem?" he asks. I've been regretting that I let the pastor limit the number of speakers at the funeral service. Thinking I should have been more forceful.

"Yes," I say.

He takes his position with the other pallbearers. The pastor leads the way as they carry the casket to the metal stand that sits on the fake grass over the big hole.

The pastor stands over the coffin and says words that come out in a mumble. Maybe I can't hear him over the wind, over the rush in my ears. Or maybe he cannot enunciate in the cold. My eyes don't leave the casket.

Then Chris reads, clear and strong.

> "Ryan,
> I can't hide these tears I shed for you.
> The love of a friend will always be true.
> True to the last drop of blood, the last thought of pain,
> true forever, even after you're gone.
> Feelings never change.
> So much sadness and sorrow,
> I wish I could borrow
> a few minutes of God's time
> so I can see you tomorrow . . ."

The crowd is hushed as he continues reading. No one says anything when the poem ends, stunned by the simple beauty of it. The vocals of the band Outlet play in the background.

"Beautiful," I say to Chris.

The pastor steps forward. "We therefore commit Ryan's body to the ground—"

The pastor's words are distinct now. "—earth to earth, ashes to ashes, dust to dust—"

"No!" I try to expel a new vision of Ryan. My handsome boy. Ashes and dust? I collapse on top of the casket. "No. Ryan. No."

"Sher." Michael's breath is on my ear, his hands on my shoulders.

I clutch the coffin all the more tightly. "Nooooo," I wail, hugging that box as only a desperate mother will do. In a protective hold I once pledged would keep my son safe.

PART II
YEARNING AND ISOLATION

In Memoriam

Time can pass so slowly.
You become unaware of the sun
and you forget that birds still sing.
The headaches last all day,
into the night,
until at last sleep saves us.

We are without you.
That is what we know.
This is what we have become.
Yesterday you were here;
today we visit your grave.
This pain cuts short our own precious lives.

Ryan, I miss you so much.
No words can express the deep emptiness I feel.
Regrets over simple sibling rivalries,
never telling you how very much I love you.

Today would be your birthday.
I am just so sorry for you;
so very sorry that you cannot be home with us today.

I love you always,
your big sister,
–Am

TIME

Time is now broken into stretches between anniversaries. Each morning I startle awake immediately before the time of The Phone Call, check the clock, and wait for it. And then I wait for the hour of Ryan's death. Count the minutes. Relive the time spent between The Phone Call and the pronouncement, "I'm sorry. He rallied there for a while."

I count the days. This is the first day, the second day, the third day after The Phone Call. I have said to myself, "Yesterday Ryan was alive." "Two days ago Ryan was alive." This morning I said, "One week ago Ryan was alive."

As time passes, it brings no solace. It steals the familiar. The lingering scents, the fresh history, the clear memory. It is persistent in its forging ahead. It pulls Ryan backward and pushes me forward, widening the distance between us. I meet it with a resistance that wearies me.

I want to grab time by the shoulders and force it to march in the opposite direction. To retrace its steps back to that night, to those chance decisions, that random series of missteps. I plead for an opportunity to change just one little thing for a different result.

Everything was perfect at one moment in time, and at this

other point, it wasn't. He had lobster for dinner, and then he got a phone call. He almost didn't go out, but then he went to a friend's party. I almost called him, but then I didn't. He got into the passenger seat of someone's car, and the car crashed.

I will never, ever see Ryan again.

I am desperate to change it.

AND TIME AGAIN

The cemetery beckons again, like it did the first time I visited today. And the second. I can't help myself. I am restless with the worry that Ryan is lonely. That kid loved a crowd.

A stomach flop catches in my throat as it always does when I turn into the cemetery. I look for recent tire tracks. I peer through the driver's side window as I pull up to Ryan's grave, searching for evidence that someone has been here. My eyes scan the aging mound of bouquets and the flat steel marker, looking for a fresh flower, a special stone, a lit candle. Nothing new. Not since the last time I was here two hours ago.

"Well, at least you have the nameplate," I comfort myself, thinking back to when we first returned to the cemetery following the graveside service and I realized there was nothing to mark Ryan's grave. Just the dirt and the flowers.

"What will mark his grave?" I asked Bart.

"Nothing," he said. "Until you get a monument."

"Nothing? There can't be nothing. Nothing?"

"I'll get you something," Bart promised.

A few hours later, he brought us a temporary little marker with Ryan's name and dates on it. A galvanized steel faceplate with stakes on the underside that one can secure by kicking it into the frozen ground. But to do so would require someone's boot to slam repeatedly on Ryan's name. We left Bart to install it, unable to bear witness to the pounding on Ryan's name.

"I know it's not enough," I assure Ryan, looking at the marker now set at the head of Ryan's grave with the glass-jar candle centered right above it. The flame has gone out again. I grab the matches from the vehicle's console. We have to keep the candle lit.

Walking around the disturbed ground to the candle, I kneel down and strike a match to light it.

"Maybe we'll get you a tree," I say aloud to shove away the silence. As soon as the words escape I feel some relief at having a new chore to do for Ryan. A mother can't stop mothering just like that. Just because her son will never come home again. Just because he lies six feet beneath the surface of the ground.

"A live one," I tell him. "Then we can plant it for you in the spring."

I adjust the protective cup of my left hand as I strike another match. Then another. The matches won't stay lit long enough to relight the candle.

"And we need to get something for the top of those columns," I say to Ryan, striking match after match between words now. "At." Strike. "The." Strike. "Entrance." Strike. The wind extinguishes each match after an initial burst of flame.

"Please?" There is a pinch in my neck as I look up to the sky. "I just need to keep his candle lit." I beseech a God who has never answered me. "Please let me do this one thing for him." In the silence that follows I bow my head and weep.

A tear rolls down my nose, drops onto the matchbook. I fling the matches into the wind as hard as I can and collapse my full body onto the frozen ground, lying prone. A shivering mass of futility.

Oh, Ryan. I'm trying. I really am trying, Ryan. I turn onto my right side and run the ungloved fingertips of my left hand over the raised letters on his marker, tracing the R, the Y, the A, the N.

A black pickup truck comes into my line of vision, creeping down the roadway that will curve around to bring it to where I am parked. I must be quite the sight lying here like this. The chill has numbed me, making it hard to stand. I manage to push myself onto my knees. My fingers don't want to bend at the knuckles, making it harder than it should be to pick up the burned matches on the ground in front of me. To grip them, to maneuver them into my coat pocket. I use my hands to thrust myself onto my feet, one painful movement at a time.

I keep my eyes to the ground and my back to the truck as it rolls past. The matchbook I threw earlier sits atop the snow about three feet away, marring the landscape. I take a step to retrieve it.

The truck exits the cemetery without stopping. A silent witness. I wonder if it was one of Ryan's friends and feel bad for subjecting whoever it was to the image of my writhing on the ground. *Sorry.*

Retrieved matchbook in hand, I pause at Ryan's grave and tell him, "I have to find out about those eternal flames," before heading back to the car.

WHERE IS UNCLE RYAN?

"Where is Uncle Ryan?" Kalum asks. The dreaded question. I notice he's the only one in the house who speaks in a normal tone now. The rest of us whisper. Even the dogs are more subdued. It's like Ryan's vitality gathered up all its friends in the household and walked out the door. Took a road trip. Only Kalum's energy decided to stick around.

"Where?" Kalum insists, not accustomed to having his questions ignored.

I'm wondering how to explain the inexplicable to a not-quite-three-year-old.

"I don't know," Amber finally responds. "He's not here."

"What do you want for lunch?" I ask, even though I cannot stomach any nourishment myself. Thinking I must be breaking all the rules on how to handle this sort of thing, I push up from the chair where I'd been staring into the distance at nothing. "Soup or a sandwich?"

Now my questions go ignored.

Amber and Kalum are looking at one another. I am looking at them. I glance at Michael to see he is observing them as well.

Amber and Kalum spend every day here now. We need to be together. I'm afraid to let them out of my sight because if Ryan can die then no one is safe. How can you have two children one day, and then the next day only one? And if that can happen, then the one can just as quickly be reduced to none. The sheer terror of it stirs my stomach.

"I think Uncle Ryan was in a car crash," Kalum says.

Amber nods her head.

But no one answers the question, "Where is Uncle Ryan?" I can't think of a more honest response than Amber's. We just don't know. He's not here.

INVESTIGATION

"What's happening?" I ask the state trooper. He looks uncomfortable sitting on the couch in our living room opposite Michael and me. Nervous, yet very straight and proper. *He's so young.* I feel a twinge of empathy. *This must be difficult for him.*

"We're still investigating," Trooper Miller responds.

Nine days later and they're still investigating? I'm beginning to realize how naïve I am.

"I'm taking the statements of everyone who saw Ryan in the twenty-four hours prior to, well . . ." Trooper Miller pauses and clears his throat. "uh . . . prior to his death," he says. "We're interviewing everyone. I'll be requesting a warrant for toxicology tests on the driver."

He hasn't even requested a warrant for toxicology tests yet? It's dawning on me that the investigation may take some time.

The trooper asks for Michael's statement. He doesn't need mine, he says, because I didn't see Ryan that last day. Ryan had left the house early in the morning before I was up and left again while I was still at work.

"But I heard him," I tell the trooper. "I heard Ryan playing with Kalum when I was on the phone with Amber." My voice is pleading. A mother begging for her last words.

"That isn't necessary to the investigation," he says and turns to Michael.

HOLIDAYS

Michael tosses the mail on the counter. We watch the holiday cards separate from the sympathy cards, sprawling in different directions like opposing magnetic poles. It isn't difficult to tell which is which. A red envelope falls from the kitchen counter onto the floor. It draws our eyes, but neither of us moves to retrieve it.

"They don't mean anything by it," Michael says. "They just don't realize."

"I know."

"Should we send out the Christmas cards?" Michael asks, a creature of habit and obligation.

I shake my head. The season's jubilation feels like torment, every cheerful holiday greeting an assault. The good wishes, the smiling family photographs, the newsletters from families intact. They rip my heart. "I can't even bear to look at those cards," I say, bending down to retrieve the red envelope.

"And how would we sign them?" I ask, tossing the card onto the counter to join the rest, thinking of how hard it is to suddenly drop a name from a Christmas card.

The door bursts open. "Nana! Grandpa! I'm here." Kalum

stomps his snow boots on the mat at the front entry before charging into the kitchen. "Hi!" Big smile on his face.

"Hi, Kalum," we say in unison, both trying to add some cheer to our voices. I hoist him into my arms and give him a kiss on a flushed rosy cheek.

"How are you?" I ask, removing his knit cap to free a mop of buttercream blond hair.

"Good," he says, then kicks his feet to indicate he wants down. Amber joins us at the counter as I release Kalum. Her demeanor contrasts completely with Kalum's. Her face is drawn, her long hair knotted and unkempt. I reach out and brush a wayward strand, recognize the pool in her eyes.

"Nana, do we have Christmas lights?" Kalum has found his way to the tree that has stood dark since Ryan's death. He stands before it. Assessing it.

"Yes, we have Christmas lights," I answer.

"I want the lights on," he says, and he walks over and plugs the cord into the socket with all the obstinacy of a two-and-three-quarters-year-old.

"There," Kalum says with a self-satisfied nod. He places his hands on his hips, looking like an older version of himself. The tree now awash in color.

We are slow to react. I apologize to Ryan. *I'm sorry.* It feels like a betrayal. But how can you deny a child a Christmas?

"You're not supposed to touch plugs," Michael says. "Next time ask someone to help you."

Kalum doesn't respond to the chastising.

My eyes burn. I want to cry. To busy myself I gather up the mail from the counter, separate the Christmas cards from the letters of sympathy, and pitch the unopened holiday cards into the recycle bin.

I'm sorry Ryan. I wanted a dark Christmas.

SYMPATHY CARDS

"*L*ook at this one," Michael hands me the letter he's been reading, along with the card it was enclosed in. It's from a woman we've never met. A friend of a friend.

"I wanted to extend to you my most sincere sympathy right away. I know that no loss is like your own, but sadly, I do understand. We lost our own darling Ryan in an automobile accident."

I hold the letter awhile after reading it. Knowing there are others out there who have experienced this, who understand, provides some solace. "That's nice," I say, folding the letter back into the card. "That people we don't even know take the time to write."

"Yes," Michael agrees, reaching for the card I'm handing back to him. "It really is."

He's assumed the chore of responding to expressions of sympathy. The few times I've tried I sat for painfully long periods, pen in hand, staring at a blank thank you card. Fallout from Ryan's death. My brain has turned to slush. I've forgotten how to embellish the way one should when saying thank you.

We've been saving the sympathy cards and letters and there are a few I read again and again. Those from family members and friends, those from Ryan's friends. And those from others who have lost children. I pick out Austin's card from the rose-print storage box on the kitchen counter meant for photos and videos.

Austin, who I know only vaguely from work, lost his seventeen-year-old son Adrian in a car crash less than two years ago. "My heart goes out to you and your family. You have now joined and become a member of the club that no one wishes to belong to. Those of us who have lost a child."

I remove the card from Marla. "Sherry, I honestly know what you are going through because I lost my beloved son three years ago. He was eighteen and died in an extremely freak accident. I am sharing this with you because I want you to know that even though it feels like it, you are not alone. I am here for you—if you ever want to talk, cry, scream or just be held and comforted."

The letter from Patsey. "I know what you are going through."

And the card from Maria. "Hearing the news really hit home for me as I lost my younger brother in a car accident . . . May it help you to know that others share your experience and have sustained."

Reading the words of other bereaved parents and family members somehow makes me feel less alone. Even though they have no hope to offer, they understand.

"So many people have lost children," I say to Michael for the umpteenth time.

IS THAT YOU RYAN?

I stretch my back as if adjusting my posture and lean forward, craning my neck to the right to get a first glimpse of the blue spruce. Michael turns the Nissan between the stone columns into the cemetery. The wind howls as fierce as it has all night. It is a bitter white-sky morning.

The relief feels like someone's lifted a lead blanket from my chest. "It's still standing," I announce. The live Christmas tree just north of Ryan's nameplate has suffered some wind damage. It tilts to the left, but the five-gallon bucket of rocks we used to stabilize the tree's root ball has held its ground.

"And his memorial card is still there," I add. The four-by-six-inch card bearing Ryan's photograph that I encased in leaded glass hangs like an ornament askew. As we drive closer, I am surprised to see most of the angels are intact. Only one broken angel has fallen. The golden star we are always centering above Ryan's photo is gone though. I look around for the tree skirt we used to disguise the bucket. "We need a new star," I babble at Michael as he brings the Xterra to a stop at the side of the roadway next to Ryan's grave. "And a tree skirt." Michael looks at me and sighs. An expression of helplessness and exhaustion. I know the dark rings under his eyes mirror my own.

All night long, we were side-by-side, sleepless and still. Michael feared Ryan's tree would topple, and I was afraid his memorial card and the angel ornaments would smash to the ground. We didn't want to worry each other, so we didn't share our fears until morning.

"I couldn't sleep at all last night," I said.

"Me neither," Michael replied. "The wind."

"Yeah, the cemetery," I said. Michael nodded.

Now here we are to evaluate the damage and set things right again.

We sit quietly for a moment in the warmth of the heated vehicle, too weary to move, listening to the scream of the wind. *Is that you, Ryan?* The thought crosses my mind though I don't believe in such things, having been raised by empirical evidence. Suckled by science and reason.

"Okay," I sigh aloud, offering myself encouragement. We each reach for our respective car door handles. I press my shoulder into the passenger door to push it open and squeeze through. The car door slams shut behind me.

Michael examines the bucket of stones and the tree's root ball. I fix Ryan's twisted memorial card so the photo side faces out again, then readjust the angel ornaments that Ryan's friends have added to the tree. Ryan's memorial plate is covered in a snowdrift.

"Stop erasing his name," I tell the snow and wipe it away with a gloved hand. I pick up the pieces of a broken angel from the ground and examine it, wondering if I can fix it. I place the shattered angel into the pocket of my ski jacket and look up to see Michael observing me. Tears are running down his face. I'm not sure if he's crying or if it's the wind. He reaches out and pulls me to him in a hug.

We clutch each other as if we are one, trying to cling to what once was, yet I have never felt more alone.

CHRISTMAS DAY

◈

"Bye!" Michael and I are standing in the doorway, waving goodbye to the tail end of Amber's Subaru. She maneuvers carefully on the soft blanket of fresh snow in the driveway.

"Okay, let's take it down." I don't have to tell Michael what "it" is. He knows I am referring to the Christmas tree.

"I'll get the boxes," he says and heads upstairs to the attic.

I can hardly bear the day. It feels like the length of a thousand days born out in one protracted nanosecond after another. I want to escape, but there is nowhere to run to that Ryan's absence cannot follow.

This Christmas could not have been more different from years past. We broke long intervals of silence with false attempts at louder-than-necessary gaiety and heartiness as we assembled Kalum's toys. We bought him the biggest and brightest toys we could find. A climb-in netted ball pit with a basketball hoop on one end and cheerfully colored plastic balls. A battery-run quad. Pat brought him a gigantic teddy bear. But we forgot the Christmas music. And there was none of the light laughter that usually marks the day. Like last year when we joked that Ryan's Christmas shopping entailed a short walk down a single store aisle to pick up a juicer for me, a George Foreman grill for Amber, and a crock pot for Michael. Well, that one aisle and then a toy store where he bought Kalum an armload of age-appropriate toys. Kalum's response to talking Elmo had us roaring. He refused even to touch it and poor Elmo became a dog toy instead. One year ago today. Twelve months. Fifty-two weeks. Three hundred and sixty-five days. What a difference a year makes.

I unplug the Christmas lights and my gaze again lands on the wrapped presents still underneath it. They demand attention in their bold and cheerful attire. Red and green and gold with coordinating ribbons and bows. A video game Ryan had asked for. Some tools he wanted. The traditional warm winter socks I buy everyone every year whether they want them or not. How innocent and optimistic I was when I wrapped those presents for Ryan. Just three weeks ago. Twenty-one days. How foolish.

What will we do with these presents now that Ryan is not here to open them? It occurs to me that the saddest questions in the world are among those that can't be answered. I turn from the tree and collapse onto the sofa. Bend my body in half. Rest my arms on my knees. Press my forehead into the fold. The intensity of the love and the longing and the despair combine to render me powerless.

I hear Michael's journey down the stairs, and then the drop of the empty boxes. See the top of his loafers as he steps closer to me. Feel his hand on my back.

"Ryan's presents," I manage. My head aches. I lift my face to my husband thinking there is nothing more bereft than a wrapped Christmas present that never will be opened.

"He'll never get to open them." A teardrop makes its way down my left cheek.

Nanauk walks over and rests her chin on my leg, turns her sympathetic brown eyes up to my face.

Michael's sigh is heavy. I've been noticing we sigh a lot now.

Sigh and whisper. I give Nanauk a pet on the head. "Hey girl," I say with pretend lightness.

"I have to go lie down." I cup Nanauk's chin and lift her head from my lap. Every movement demands colossal effort. Getting up from the couch. Walking up the stairs. Turning into the bedroom. *One step at a time*, I tell myself.

The sound of Michael dismantling the tree filters up to me as I acknowledge another regret.

Oh, Ryan. I wish I had given you your Christmas presents.

I'm accumulating regrets like a hoarder. The pile gets larger by the day. This regret lands atop the others. That I worked late that night. *He might still be alive.* That I let him eat his lobster before I got home. *He might still be alive.* That I didn't make a phone call. *He might still be alive.* The words beat their way into my head like a jack-hammer. *He might still be alive.* I smother my face in my pillow to silence the keening that comes from somewhere deep within the pit of me.

THE SOUND OF SILENCE

"It's quiet," I say aloud, just to hear the sound of it. Michael and Amber have returned to their regular work schedules and aside from the dogs and Tigger, our elderly tabby cat, I am often the only one home.

"It's too quiet now, isn't it Nova?" I address her sprawled bulk in front of the fireplace on the living room floor. Even the sound of my voice is hushed, somehow magnifying the stillness. Nova moves her eyes to my face without lifting her head. We are all so lethargic now. Our own lives deadened. "Poor Nova." I squat down to caress the side of her head. I wonder if she lugs around the same persistent deep ache in her chest that I carry.

There is a nudge at my back. "You too, Nanauk." I turn around to pat Nanauk's head. Like children, you must give them equal attention.

"Okay." I heft myself up. "Who wants a treat?" Nanauk follows me to the pantry, past the photo collages of Ryan that Amber and Melissa made for the wake. Prominent fixtures in our living room now. Nova, the chubbier dog who loves a treat, doesn't move. The sound of Nanauk's nails tap-tapping on the wood floor behind me is almost worse than complete silence. Hollow and empty. I wish the phone would ring, but I don't want to talk to anyone. I wish Ryan's music was blaring, but music brings me to tears. *I wish, I wish, I wish.*

Nanauk trails me back past Ryan's photo boards to Nova. "Here you go." I am about to hand the dogs their treats simultaneously when I realize the treats are shaped like bones. I can't release them fast enough. They fall to the floor. Nanauk snatches up the bone that lands nearest her. Nova considers the treat that's fallen just north of her snout before stretching her neck out to draw it into her mouth with her tongue.

The image of a skeleton gets stuck in my head and I can't shake it out. I make a mental note to tell Michael not to buy dog treats that look like bones.

FOR THE WANT OF HIM

Ryan smiles at me through each photograph in the poster-size collages, just as he did when I held the camera. I search the face of three-year-old Ryan celebrating his birthday. Look for answers in his enormous smile, the spiky blond hair sticking out from under his Ghostbusters hat.

The memory of a trip to Hartford surfaces. We drove past the old G. Fox building looming on one side of Main Street and Christ Church Cathedral with its spires reaching into the sky on the other.

"Mommy," Ryan said with breathless awe. "Look! Castles!" Life was magical back then. Full of possibility.

Oh, Ryan. The memory hurts. It's too sweet, the contrast with today intolerable. But how do you attach meaning to a person's life if the memories are lost?

And so. I scrutinize each photograph and welcome the memory. Four-year-old Ryan with his moussed-up hair sitting on a boulder just off the Appalachian trail in Virginia. Five-year-old Ryan in his life jacket at the lake preparing to go out on the sailboat. Eight-year-old Ryan wearing the sweatshirt that reads "Happiness" on the front. Ryan in his scout uniform. I examine each photograph, putting it in the context of time and place. Preserving it. I talk to him. *I love you, Ryan.*

I speak to the ten-year-old Ryan who sits studious on the couch reading under the light of the stained-glass lampshade it took me six months to make. His hair a light milk chocolate by then. Ryan in his white Tae Kwon Do uniform wrapped in a newly earned brown belt. *You enriched my life, Ryan.* I turn to the twelve-year-old Ryan standing on the back deck overlooking the lake holding up a bass that stretches from his head to his waist. Remember the day Ryan found the poor thing floating in the water, probably the recent victim of a boating accident. But it was bigger than any fish Ryan had ever pulled out of that lake. "Get the camera!" Ryan shouted. "I gotta have a picture of this."

I pull my attention from one photograph to the next. The thirteen-year-old Ryan in his backward baseball cap hugging his new puppy Nova, cheek-to-cheek. The fourteen-year-old Ryan rollerblading down the boardwalk at Hampton Beach in his tie-dyed T-shirt. The fifteen-year-old Ryan standing in front of the Wave Runner. The sixteen-year-old Ryan tenderly holding his new nephew, Kalum. The photo of a proud Ryan escorting me down the aisle of the church to deliver me to Michael. Ryan with an older Nova and an older Kalum. And then that last photograph I took of the family.

Ryan's face tells its own story in each picture. Playful, adventurous, tender, loving, happy, proud. *Oh, Ryan.*

Please, God. I will do anything. I promise, promise, promise, if only you bring him back.

NIGHTMARES

Someone grabs me, subduing me. I can no longer run.

"Shhh." I am slow to realize it is Michael holding me down and not something I have to fight. "It's okay," he says. "It's okay."

I try to pull myself out of the nightmare that battles with Michael to hold me in its clutches. Slowly my heart calms and I repeat Michael's words to him. "It's okay." I gently push him away. I have to be free of any restraint before I can remove myself from the horror of the nightmare completely.

"The same dream?" Michael's words are more of a statement than a question. I cannot answer immediately. I kick the covers free to let the cool air lap up the perspiration from my body, the last of the evidence.

"Yes," I finally respond. Michael is almost as familiar with the nightmare now as if it were his own. I am searching and searching for Ryan's legs. He cannot come home until I find his legs and I need to find them soon or it will be too late. I am running. Running in narrow alleyways, foreign places, looking in every dark corner for Ryan's legs. And I am scared. More frightened than I have ever been. If I don't find his legs he will be gone forever.

And then suddenly I can't run anymore. I am on my back and my own legs are strapped in steel braces, rendering them useless. A bar spanning from ankle to ankle forces them apart. I struggle hard, with all my might, to keep searching, but I cannot move my legs so I thrash and scream in protest. Just as I did as a child. Fighting those leg braces with all the power of a one, two, three, four, five-year-old. To walk, to run, to be liked, to fit in. But now in a battle to find Ryan's legs.

It is always at this point that I awaken to Michael holding me. "Shhh," he says. "Shhh. It's okay."

The furthest thing from the truth.

RYAN'S LEGS

"What happened to his legs?" Pat asked a day or two after seeing Ryan in the hospital.

"I don't know," I winced, trying to force the image out.

"The sheet was flat where his legs—"

"I know," I interrupted him. He'd said the words I was afraid to say, brought back the image my mind didn't want to revisit.

And now, several weeks later, I am having these nightmares. It's impossible to suppress something entirely. I've been inquiring, without outright asking, trying to assure myself Ryan had his legs. The risk is, I will find out he lost his legs in the crash, and I will spend a lifetime of nightmares searching for Ryan's legs. I probe carefully.

"Oh, God," I worried at Michael. "I don't remember bringing Ryan's shoes to the funeral director for the wake."

"I brought them," he said. "His black leather dress shoes."

"Are you sure?"

"Yes, I'm positive. Go look in his closet. You won't find them there."

I did look in Ryan's closet, and for a while I could tell myself that if we brought Ryan's shoes to the funeral home, he surely must have had his legs. Right? Feet at the end to place his shoes on.

But why was the bottom half of the casket closed? And at the hospital, why did Pat and I both see a flat sheet where Ryan's legs should have been?

Now another idea is forming. I drag myself out of bed, into the kitchen for a cup of coffee. Michael is reading the newspaper in the dining room.

"Hi, honey," he puts the paper down on the table and joins me in the kitchen. Kisses the top of my head.

"I've been wondering," I begin, pause. "Do you think you can you ask Bart if Ryan had his legs? And tell me if he did have his legs, but not tell me if he didn't?"

Michael steps back and assesses my face before answering. "I can do that," he says.

RETURN TO WORK

I wake in the shadow of some dream I can't retrieve, leaving me with a fleeting belief that Ryan is still alive. The slow rise to consciousness brings with it an awareness that staggers me for a moment. But only for a moment. *Ryan is dead.*

I turn to Michael's empty side of the bed and check the time. *Ugh. I have to get up.* Instead, I plop back down and stare at the ceiling fan. *How can I do this?* I don't know how I will manage this first day back to work when every movement takes so much effort. When every step seems impossible. When I've lost all ability to concentrate. When I don't know how to feign normalcy. As if my family were intact. *Move one foot.* I urge myself. *Then the other.* I sit up. I swing my legs over the side of the bed. I stand.

My trepidation at having to resume a normal routine stays with me as I get ready. As I brush my teeth. As I place my left foot into the leg of my black slacks. And then my right. As I realize I've lost a good deal of weight since I last wore these pants. As I rummage the closet for a belt. Every small chore seems to take forever. I feel like I'm in some altered universe where I've got to slog through quicksand to do any little thing.

The crying starts on the drive to work. I am doing something routine for the first time since Ryan died just over a month ago. One month and one day ago. Four weeks and four days ago. Thirty-two days ago. I am going to work as I always did on weekdays when Ryan was alive. Back to normal, like Ryan's death didn't change everything. *But it did,* I insist, as Guilt with a capital G merges with the pile of regrets to snuggle a little closer. *I'm sorry, Ryan.*

∼

THERE IS a tentative knocking on the closed door of my office, something I both expect and dread as I sit bawling at my desk.

Please, not yet, shaking my head. *I can't do this right now.*

Another hesitant knock. *Damn.*

"Yes?" I answer. No one responds and I realize the word was too small to be heard. *Maybe they will go away,* I think, recognizing immediately how unfair I am being. Everyone has been so good to me.

This day has been an exercise in determination. Pulling myself from sleep, telling myself I have to get up, I have to get dressed, I have to go to work. Battling with the part of me who wants to do none of these things. The part of me who wants to sleep forever. Who will win? Even I don't know. The me who wants to give up and die sinks back into myself for a while. The me who must go on gathers courage.

"Come in," I finally offer with more determination.

My office door opens as if it too is uncertain. Faye, my supervisor and lead lawyer of the Intellectual Property & Technology practice group, steps in. She closes the door behind her.

"How are you?" Faye asks. I notice concern has made its mark on her face, just as she must notice grief has made its mark on mine.

"I'm sorry," I say. "I know I should—"

"No," she stops me.

"I want him back," I tell her. "I just want him back," I sob, repeating those words over and over.

When Faye leaves, closing my office door behind her, I cross my arms on top of my desk and lay my forehead down. Close my eyes. Let the tears and saliva merge, puddle on the desk beneath my face. *I want you back Ryan. Please, Ryan, come back.*

Another knock.

"Yes?" My voice has a hard time traveling through the debris. I lift my head. A tall man with gentle eyes and toffee skin looms in the doorway.

"Hi," he says as he steps into my office. "I'm Austin."

"Oh Austin." I know Austin from the sympathy card he sent. One of those I've read again and again. He's the father of Adrian, who was killed in a crash not quite two years ago. I am out of my chair, hugging him, and in this instant he becomes my brother, though we have only seen each other in passing before now.

"How are you?" he asks. I don't know how to respond and burst into a fresh stream of tears.

"I want him back," I say. "I just want him back." A broken record.

"I know," he responds.

"I'm sorry. For you. That you have suffered this too," I say. "How do you do it? How do you go on?"

"I don't know." His voice conveys sadness and resignation. "We just do. Either that or we die ourselves." He looks for a long moment at my face. "Maybe you're not ready to return to work yet."

∽

ANOTHER TAP at my office door comes about an hour later. I open it to see Faye again, weighed down with a stack of files in her arms.

"Here," she says, offering me the pile. "I want you to work on these files from home."

The relief is immediate. "Thank you."

"Stay in touch," she says, "and let me know when you're ready to come back."

FALLEN ANGELS OR RESURRECTION

Both dogs startle when I slap the work file closed and plop it atop the pile of other files stacked on the desk. My ability to concentrate, to hold a thought that doesn't involve Ryan or worry for Amber and Kalum and Michael, has gone missing. Work, like almost everything else, feels insignificant. But I am grateful for the time to work from home at my own pace, so I make the effort.

It's only me with the dogs, a drowsy old cat, and my thoughts during the day. I write. I work. I visit the cemetery. I take steps to establish a charity in Ryan's name and wander the house fantasizing about memorials for him. I may visit the cemetery again. Light a candle. Shovel the snow from the roadside to his grave. Look for signs of other visitors and fallen angels. I'm always resurrecting fallen angels. Gluing broken wings back together. Placing restored angels in protective locations on Ryan's tree.

Sometimes I watch Kalum while his parents are at work. I'm careful not to lay my grief on him, but that may be impossible. This is what I've been thinking since Tuesday when Amber came to pick him up. She asked Kalum what he had done that day.

"Me and Nana went to the cemetery," he said, grabbing his coat.

"But what else did we do?" I asked, encouraging him to share our trip to the library. The book I read to him. The tacos and guacamole we had for lunch at a favorite Mexican restaurant. The puzzle we put together.

"We went to the cemetery again," Kalum responded, swinging the bangs from his eyes with a sharp sweep of his head.

"Well, yes, but—"

Amber dipped her chin and raised her eyebrows at me.

"We did a lot of other things too though," I said, feeling both chastised and disappointed in myself. What stood out in Kalum's memory of the day were the two trips to the cemetery. *I can't do anything right.*

And that's how I feel when I slap my work file closed. *I can't do anything right.*

It takes both arms to heft myself up from the chair. Nova and Nanauk hoist themselves to stand with me. My constant companions. Every movement each of us makes is a battle.

The dogs are at my heels as I work my way to the closed door of Ryan's bedroom, hesitate a moment, then turn the knob, and step into the room.

PRESERVATION

His scent is fading, I admit to myself as I take another step into Ryan's bedroom, then immediately try to push the thought aside and control the panic. That earthy-boy-cologne combination I love. Fresh air, garden soil and Old Spice. Now hardly discernible. I take a deep breath, trying to capture what is left of him, and usher the dogs out of the room before closing the door. I need to preserve his scent. What will I do when that too leaves me?

The view outside Ryan's back window beckons. This is what greeted him each morning. In warmer months, the pond and waterfall surrounded by flower gardens and fieldstone patios. The white picket fence guarding the vegetable garden. The songbirds at the feeder. Now a black-and-white photograph, but beautiful in its winter starkness. A red cardinal lands on the feeder reminding me there is still color in this world.

"Maybe we can bring you back here," I say aloud, forcing some sound into the house. "Have you buried here. Surrounded by the things you love instead of in that bitter cold cemetery." *That wind pocket of a cemetery. Abuser of angels and candle flames.* I settle on the bed, feeling a renewed sense of purpose at having another thing to do for Ryan. I like this idea of a family cemetery on our property.

Everything in Ryan's room is how he left it. His bed is set against the walls that form a corner under the windows facing south and east. His hat collection gazes outward from the rustic hat tree Mike made him for Christmas one year. A Grateful Dead poster hangs on the wall above Ryan's desk and computer. His television and stereo sit at mute attention in the entertainment center opposite his bed. All of Ryan's belongings seem to anticipate the boy. Nothing has changed. *Except for Ryan's scent*, I acknowledge, *escaping from every nook and cranny.*

I grab Ryan's pillow and smother my face in it. *He is here*, I tell myself, comforted. *He is still here.*

But I don't hold the pillow to my face for long. If I do, Ryan's scent will be replaced by my own. Like the Enyce shirt of his I wear now. I return the pillow to the head of Ryan's bed, setting it just right, and continue to scrutinize his things.

Ryan's shoe catches my eye for the zillionth time. That white Reebok with the bit of dried mud on it sitting next to its pristine mate, toes to the wall. Like a magnet, that shoe always draws my attention.

Ryan wouldn't want the dirt there, so meticulous that kid was with his shoes. I almost smile at the thought. My urge is to wipe it, but I stop myself each time. Something must have brushed Ryan's shoe as he took a step, as he moved in his certain way, causing that mud to be there.

So I leave it. Unable to wipe away that little indication of the way my son once moved.

LESS DECORATED

Back in my own bedroom, I resume the task I started earlier in the week. Getting rid of everything colorful and flamboyant about me. All my funky jewelry and clothing. I assess what remains of my earrings and grab the pair of large gold and turquoise sailboats. I can't help but hold them up to eye level and pause a moment to appreciate them for the last time before dropping them into a box destined for the Salvation Army. I release them and watch them settle atop the pile. They were my favorite.

The irony is not lost on me. All of Ryan's belongings are intact, his room as he left it, his clothes in the closet, his truck in the driveway. It is my things I am tossing. I can't wipe a bit of dried mud from Ryan's shoe, yet I can discard everything that was fun about me without a care.

I have stripped myself of color and music. Of decoration and sound. Of regular nourishment. I feel the life draining from my mind and body and there is no way to stop it.

COMPASSIONATE FRIENDS

I come to a complete stop, standing in the hallway outside the open door that seems more like an obstacle than something that beckons. It carries me back in time to that other open doorway in the hospital that I breached.

The twenty or so people in the room are sitting in chairs that circle a small table topped with Kleenex tissues and a lit candle sitting in the center.

Marla, who brought me here, is by my side. I am about to attend my first meeting of The Compassionate Friends, an organization of parents whose children have died. Now that I see them, all these parents of dead children, the last thing I want is to belong to this group.

"I can't." Tears stream down my face. "I can't do this," I repeat over and over, shaking my head. Marla is gentle with me. She doesn't insist, but merely stands by my side, pats me, hugs me. I gather strength in her touch, in the fragrance of her wavy shoulder-length chestnut brown hair, in the deep compassion of her liquid root beer eyes.

"I know," she says. And in those two spoken words, I find a camaraderie I suddenly realize will last a lifetime. Even though we only recently met. Even though we had only corresponded via email until now. Marla does know. Her beautiful teenage son Josh died in a drowning accident three years ago.

Crying hard now with great heaving gasps of air, I let Marla take my hand and we walk through the door, from one world into the next. From the past into the future. From solitude to solidarity.

Someone offers a few welcoming remarks. I don't hear the sounds as words, but as a calming voice. And then one-by-one, each person in the circle of chairs talks, explains why they are here.

"My son went to the hospital for routine surgery and he never came out. He was ten."

I hear children's names: Michelle, Andrew, Rico.

And I hear words such as leukemia and suicide and motorcycle crash.

Then it is someone's turn who is crying as hard as I am and cannot speak. The woman next to her says, "She can't. My nephew, Danny, her son, died in a car crash along with two of his high school friends on December 6." She pauses before adding, "It's hard."

I watch as the distance between the person speaking and me grows shorter and shorter. Then it is my turn. "My son," I can scarcely get it out. "Ryan. My only son." Marla places her hand on my knee. "He was killed in a car crash on December 7. He was a passenger in a car with two other kids. He's the only one who . . . my baby." It is all I can manage through a fresh stream of tears and other secretions.

"Our son died from a drug overdose," the man with the English accent says. "On December 8."

The dates register with me. December 6, December 7, December 8. Oh, my God. I didn't know there was so much premature death in the world.

WHAT DO YOU DO WITH A THING CALLED HOPE?

I scan the surnames on the spines of the tidy white binders that fill an entire wall of my home office. Scores of ancestors are represented here. Lives captured in three rings and archival quality plastic sleeves that hold photos and letters, news articles and vital records. Lives I've reconstructed.

The absurdity is I am organizing Ryan's life in the same way. Perched cross-legged on the floor surrounded by stacks of papers and files and and binders and sheet protectors. Sitting to my right, filled with mementos and keepsakes, is Ryan's open hope chest.

Hope. *Aptly named. All you can do is hope.*

I slide one of Ryan's school papers into a sheet protector and place it in chronological order in one of the special binders that hold the contents of Ryan's life. *Thank God I saved these things.* For a moment I am awash with gratitude. *All the little notes my children wrote to me.* I grab one from the top of the pile. Ryan was ten-years-old when he wrote that he was going out to play and would check in around 3:00. He signed the note, "Love Ryan, your beautiful loving son." Then he added a P.S. "I am writing sloppy because I hurt my right arm really bad and it is badly sprained or maybe even broken." I smile, remembering how my heart dropped as I first read those words.

I sleeve and file the Christmas wish lists he gave me, sketches he drew, his baby teeth sealed in labeled envelopes. One envelope has Ryan's writing on it. "My only silver tooth, age 11. Got two bucks for it." *Thank goodness I saved all these things.*

I file Ryan's Tae Kwon Do promotion certificates and letters from girls. *I'm sorry Ryan. I read them. I couldn't help myself.*

I caress the cards he made for me, pausing over each one. "Dear mom, I hope you have a very great Mother's Day. You are the best mother in the world . . . Love, your favorite one and only son, Ryan."

Waves of helplessness and longing pass through me, the want of him is so great. How can the sweet boy who wrote these words be gone? I want to growl. I want to pound the ground in the throes of a tantrum, tell fate no, he will not be dead. I forbid it. But I've tried all these things and I know I am powerless.

"Shit," I slap the floor with the palm of my hands.

"Hate," I cry louder and strike harder.

"Fuck," I fling ugly words into the air like a pitcher might hurl fastballs. Smack the floor with each syllable.

One of the dogs whines through the closed door. *Can you let me have a moment?* I cup my hands to my face and try to empty the anger with a deep breath in and out before apologizing.

"It's okay Nova and Nanauk." I try to sound comforting. "I'm sorry. It's okay." They aren't used to being separated from me like this, but I can't have them in the room tromping all over Ryan's life.

It takes me another moment to resume the work. My eye comes to rest on one of Ryan's school papers titled, "My Future Plans."

"I am going to strike it rich, get married to a beautiful woman, and have three children," he wrote.

All that love. My grandchildren. Amber's nieces and nephews, Kalum's cousins. All that loss.

I can't sit here anymore. I push myself up off the floor, walk over to the genealogy wall and browse the alphabetically arranged typewritten surnames. It is this room that reminds me I am not on a solitary journey, that grief is a universal experience. I am not the only mother to have howled at the Heavens, to have sunk to her knees over the grave of her child.

I pull out a binder and turn the pages until I see Elizabeth, one of my great grandmothers. Six of the children she bore predeceased her. My empathy for her is so great it feels like I have a second heart that can be broken. This is not the first time I've pulled Elizabeth from the bookshelf since Ryan's death.

"How did you survive it?" I ask her, placing the open binder on the floor. Maybe her presence will give me some strength.

I turn back to Ryan, the evidence of his life. Once my future. Now my history. What do you do when your future becomes your past? And what do you do with everything that won't fit neatly into a three-ring binder? The favorite baby blanket? The first pair of doll-size jeans? The Mother's Day crafts?

You tenderly place them back into a chest called Hope. Try to shove what you can of your emotion inside. Fasten the lid. Work your way to the walk-in closet. Maneuver the chest deep into a corner.

Then, ever so gently, you turn your back and close the door on Hope.

BOOKS

"Oh, you're lucky," the librarian with the rheumatoid knuckles says.

I scan the titles of the five books I ordered through the interlibrary loan service, all involving parental bereavement. The only thing I can read now.

"No . . ." I hesitate, at a loss for words.

How do I tell her that I'm about as far removed from being lucky as a person can be? That I can't read like I used to. That an abandoned bookmark reveals the place in Victor Hugo's *Les Misérables* where I stopped reading the night before Ryan's death. A bookmark that may forever be held in the clutches of pages 652 and 653 on a shelf in a library of books in our home. Books I can't read now because grief has robbed me of concentration, of interest, of an attention span.

How do I tell her that these bereavement books are a lifeline? That they help me feel less alone. They help me understand the experience. Find words for it. That my reading life has turned upside down. From escape to immersion.

"I'm sorry," I tell the librarian. For what, I don't know, but that's what comes out.

"You hardly ever get them in all at once like this," the librarian says as she picks up the grief books, one-by-one, and proceeds with the checkout process.

"Oh," I respond. Now I get it. "Yes. All at once." *What luck*, I think to myself.

FAMILY PLOT OR HOME TURF

The letter addressed to me from the town of Coventry grabs my attention. I place the rest of the mail, mostly bills I keep forgetting to pay, on my desk and tear into the thick envelope from the town.

"I am responding to a recent phone mail message from you regarding zoning requirements for a family burial plot," the letter from the Director of Planning and Development begins. As I read further my heart plummets. It sounds like it will be nearly impossible to bring Ryan home. We will have to form a nonprofit organization and apply for a special permit from the Planning and Zoning Commission to establish a cemetery on our property. The applicable regulations are enclosed.

I release the letter so that it falls on top of the other mail and turn my back to it. Deny it. "Damn." My resignation toys with my will to fight. *It's not like I want to establish a real cemetery. All I want to do is bring my son home.* The world is battling with me at every turn and I don't have the power to mount a counterattack.

Ryan shouldn't be in that stark, wind-torn cemetery that no one knows is there. The one situated behind the other cemetery in town that everyone knows. He should be here with his family on this property that might one day have been his.

I've been thinking about that day last summer, standing with Amber and Ryan on the fieldstone patio at the rear of the house. Counting the fish in the pond. Admiring everything surrounding it. The wrap-around flower gardens were at their best. We planted them so that new blooms cycle through each month of the growing season, but mid-July is the most spectacular. One section of the garden is dedicated to all things blue. Another nurtures a multi-colored spread of blooming daylilies under the guard of the mounted bird mansion. Five-plus acres of woods and fruit trees, grapevines and blueberries. A sand volleyball court in the back meadow. How fortunate we are, I was thinking.

"Someday this will be yours," I told them, "but we'll have to figure out how to split it."

"I don't want this property," Amber said. "I want 60," she added, referring to the street number of the first little house I bought when I was twenty-something. The house we still owned that would always hold some childhood magic in Amber's eyes.

"It's a deal!" Ryan shouted. "I want that in writing. Get me a pen and paper," he said gesturing to the house. We laughed.

"I'm serious," Ryan insisted, signaling again for someone to go get him that pen and paper.

Amber and I shared a glance and stood our ground. "We don't deliver," I responded, setting off another round of giggles.

But this caused us to think about it, Michael and me. How to make a fair division.

Now, all I can do is try to bring Ryan back home. To the fruit trees and evergreens and gardens and the songbirds he woke up to. To the place he loved.

I'll do what I can to bring you home Ryan, I vow. *I'll try to bring you home.*

IT'S EVERYWHERE

We are experimenting with venturing out again. I've managed to return to work for half days. That alone takes almost everything I have. Michael suggested we resume our weekly volleyball games but I'm uncomfortable around people now, and I can hardly lift a leg to move sometimes.

"How about a movie?" Michael asks. I ignore him. He persists. "We can try a movie. Just us."

I recognize I have isolated myself and that Michael is more isolated as a result. I know we need to find our way back into the world but it's a different world and I don't know how. And I don't want to. Anything that once provided pleasure now consumes me with Guilt. How can I eat when Ryan can no longer enjoy a meal? How can I go to the theater when Ryan will never see another movie?

The memory of our first failed attempt surfaces as a warning. We had season tickets to the Hartford Stage theater and we went to see the play, *Electra*, putting no thought into it other than we would try to do something normal. The play, wrought with betrayal, grief, and revenge left me stunned. We walked out during intermission.

"Sher?" Michael snaps me out of myself.

"Maybe," I say, only because I know I can't give up. It's not fair to my family not to try.

"How about *The Lord of the Rings*?" Michael says, turning the newspaper toward me and pointing to an ad for *The Two Towers*. "We liked the first one."

"Okay," I say when what I really mean is, *I don't care*. Neither of us has the ambition or attention span to do more investigating. Ryan is dead. We pick a time and off we go.

We choose the back row at the Showcase Cinemas as we always do. I sit blindly through the previews. As the movie begins, Michael covers my hand in his. I try at first to follow the plot, but it is too complex for my post-Ryan's-death mind. I give up and stare vacantly at the screen until the King's son, Théodred, dies. Suddenly I am on high alert. King Théoden stands over his son's grave crying that no parent should have to bury a child and I am bawling right along with him.

"It's everywhere," I tell Michael as we are leaving. "Death. It's everywhere. We can't do anything without being confronted by it."

"I know," Michael agrees. And we can't get home quickly enough.

I feel a sense of relief as I open the front door. My sanctuary, safe and familiar. But as I enter the house and gaze into the living room, I see it with new eyes. The photo collages from Ryan's wake still displayed, his framed memorial card mounted on the wall, his dried roses.

Death. It's everywhere.

ON TOP OF THE WORLD

*I*n going through the photographs my eye is drawn to two in particular. The one I took on the ferry to Liberty Island with the Manhattan skyline in the background. That shot captures the teenage faces of Ryan and Amber, with the World Trade Center's twin towers almost sitting on Ryan's right shoulder in the background. Three of the four subjects in that photo gone now.

And the photo we took from the crown of the Statue of Liberty.

When we disembarked from the ferry, Amber and I had been daunted by the crowd, the line, the wait.

"Do you really want to stand in this line and then climb all the way to the crown?" I asked the kids. Amber and I were willing to abandon it, but Ryan insisted.

"I didn't come here to just walk away," Ryan said. "I'm going up."

So we all did. Climbed to the very top, up the dim, steep and narrow winding steps, wrought iron support straps mounted everywhere at odd angles. When we finally reached the heights, we looked through Miss Liberty's crown windows onto city skylines, the Hudson and East Rivers merging in the foreground, ships entering New York Harbor. Amber and I were glad Ryan had insisted.

"What an incredible view," Amber said. It was a clear, crisp, blue sky day. We all agreed.

"Welcome to America," I said to the ships below. Amber and Ryan, on either side of me, both turned to look at me as if I had said something very strange.

"What?" I asked, ready to launch into a diatribe about history and voyages and ancestors who this noble lady first welcomed to America. But the kids read my mind.

"We know, mom," Amber said in her cocky seventeen-year-old manner. I didn't even have to say anything and they knew what was coming. They snickered and I couldn't suppress a smile. *Typical mom*, I could hear them thinking.

We stood for a few moments longer in silence, pleased with ourselves for making the trip, appreciating the view, the distant skyline, the expanse of water.

"I feel like I'm on top of the world," Ryan said. We all agreed.

Reliving that day brings such a deep ache of longing I have to turn the page of the photo album.

Like closing my eyes to a memory.

The memory of being on top of the world.

INVESTIGATION IS COMPLETE

"The investigation is complete," Trooper Miller says. He looks down. Shuffles the papers in his hands. Everything about him is crisp and polished. From his close-cropped hair to his uniform to his shoes. I cannot help but evaluate him. Compare him with the man he was five months ago when he first came to our house and sat on this same couch. "You can expect an arrest within the next couple of weeks," he says. More mature. Less uncertain.

I can see he is evaluating me as well. These months have been hard on her, he must think. Twenty pounds lighter. Oversized clothing. Outgrown hair. We are wholly in contrast with one another.

I mull over his words. *An arrest.*

Michael leans into me and places his palm on my knee. Nova stretches her front legs toward the fireplace and sighs in her sleep.

"Was The Driver intoxicated?" I ask.

"Yes."

"Ryan?"

"There were trace amounts of alcohol. He'd been drinking. But he wasn't intoxicated."

I let the information sink in.

"You have been very patient," Trooper Miller adds.

Have I been patient? I don't know. I have counted the days. The one hundred and seventy-seven days it took to reach today. Two seasons. A winter and a spring. But there hasn't been room to think about the investigation with all the energy required to try to bring Ryan back. To carry him into the future. To keep him vibrant in everyone's thoughts, current in their minds.

"What are the charges?" I ask.

"Well, we're going to finalize that with the state's attorney. But definitely manslaughter."

"Oh." *Manslaughter. Manslaughter?* I practice saying the word in my mind.

"You'll be assigned a victim's advocate. The state's attorney will want your input. He'll probably be contacting you."

"Oh." I am thinking, *Ryan was killed. He's not just lost, or dead. It wasn't just an accident. He was killed.* This is a new way of thinking that leaves me at a loss for words.

"Oh."

THE RECRUITER

The phone startles me, the way it always does now. Not like when Ryan was alive and it rang constantly. Something that contributed to the din—music, voices, frisky dogs, and the phone.

It is Ryan's recruitment officer. *Recruitment officer? He had a recruitment officer?*

"Hello, ma'am. Is Ryan there?" he asks after introducing himself.

His question staggers me. I haven't heard those words in so long.

"What?" I ask. Unbelieving for a moment, not knowing what else to say.

He enthusiastically asks for Ryan again. What feels like fear buckles my insides. I have longed for Ryan's phone calls in the silence of the aftermath. But there is something alarming about getting a call like this six months after your son has died. *Be careful what you wish for.*

"Um, well, um, Ryan—" I stammer.

"Yes, can I talk to him?" I hear impatience growing in his voice.

"Uh . . . nooo."

"Do I have the proper residence?" inquired the unknowing and now too harried voice over the phone.

"Yes," I say and think, *well, kind of.* We both pause in uncomfortable silence. He, not knowing what to say to be more direct, and me not knowing how direct to be.

Ryan wanted to join the military after 9/11. He mounted a full-size American flag on his pickup truck, my patriotic boy who leaned to the conservative. One night at the dinner table he told us he wanted to join the Navy. Protect our country, he said. I dissuaded him, afraid he would be injured or killed. And just as I had talked him out of buying a motorcycle and getting a tattoo, he listened.

"Ryan's not here," I tell the recruiter. "He's dead," I add, recognizing how improper this is. But what else is there to say?

"Oh, gee," the recruiter responds.

"Can you please remove Ryan from your call list?" I ask.

"Yup, I'll remove him. Definitely. I'm sorry for your loss, ma'am."

"Thank you," softer now, in a tone that acknowledges defeat. I'm thinking I shouldn't have dissuaded Ryan from joining the military as I did.

Capital G.

He might still be alive.

COURT

My peripheral vision warns me that The Driver's lawyer is lumbering toward me as I leave the courtroom. There is no place to hide.

He comes too close. I can smell the stale coffee on his breath as he says, "I'm sorry for your loss." The Driver is behind him, looking over the wrinkle in the suit of his lawyer's left shoulder into my face.

"I appreciate that," I respond, stepping back from the foulness of the lawyer's breath. I look down and take another step away. I cannot gaze into those eyes. The Driver's eyes. Nothing much happened in court again today. Another continuance. I spent the time studying the defendant from behind, watching his demeanor from a distance, trying to assess my own feelings. I worry about what prison might do to him while my heart rejects that additional burden. What I carry is too heavy. I might not hold up under any more weight. *It's not you prosecuting him,* I tell myself. *It's the state. There's nothing you can do about it.*

"I know how you feel," the lawyer continues. "I almost lost my daughter some time back. When she was twelve years old."

The last thing I want to do is listen to the story of his almost-but-not-dead daughter. My helplessness turns to quiet anger at the comparison. Almost losing a child is nothing like actually losing a child. I raise my head, assess the dark of his oil-slicked hair, the deeply lined puffs of his pale face, the thin red-river veins mapping his nose. "No," I say, voice low and slow, looking directly into his smallish deep-set eyes. "You do not know how I feel." With those words, I find the power to release myself and flee from the courthouse before bursting into tears that have their way with me for the full half-hour it takes to get back to the office.

He does not know how I feel. I hiccup as I drive down the highway.

He does not know how I feel, I tell myself as I park the car.

Walking from the parking garage to the office, I somehow stifle the emotion. Package it up in a sturdy box, seal it with heavy-duty packing tape, stuff it way deep down somewhere. Then I square my shoulders and prepare myself to manage the trivia of the day.

GREATER HARTFORD FESTIVAL OF JAZZ OR ALL THAT JAZZ

"*D*amn," I say to myself again, thinking, *I can't believe I did that.*

I am sitting in the double wooden rocker on the stone patio behind the house staring at the fish pond. Thinking back to yesterday. Despondent.

Friends have been reaching out to us, trying to encourage us back into the social world. And we are trying. When another couple invited us to join them for the Hartford Jazz Fest, we accepted.

Bushnell Park was crowded. Everyone appeared happy to the point of exuberance. I felt like a contradiction. My clearest thought was that it was another anniversary. Thirty-two weeks exactly since Ryan's death. Seven months and twelve days. Two hundred and twenty-four days.

My warning to myself that morning was, "Don't bring everyone down, Sherry." I reminded myself of it throughout the afternoon as I tried to make light conversation. The music was good, our friends so caring. But I felt separated, even as I sat in the middle of it. A raindrop in a blaze of sunshine.

The conversation turned to our friends' children, and I suddenly realized I could never again talk about Ryan in the way parents talk about their living children. Gloating over their accomplishments, sharing silly stories, the funny things they said or did.

It came out of my mouth with no forethought or filter. I said, "I'll never be able to talk about Ryan like that now."

There was a moment of silence when I wished I could suck those words back into my lungs.

"Does it bother you when I talk about our son?"

"No, no. Of course not," I said, a dagger in my heart. How can I tell a mother not to speak of her children?

"I'll have some of that wine now," I said, turning to Michael.

I drank a glass of wine, and another, and another. False conversation came much easier. And then I was standing up and applauding the band, boisterous, big smile on my face.

The memory of it is tearing at me now. I feel disloyal to Ryan and wary at how self-administered anesthesia can temporarily numb even the deepest of wounds.

"You have to be careful," I caution myself as I take another sip of hot Earl Grey. "Very, very careful."

COMMUNITY OF BEREAVED

&

"Do you mind if I sing something?" Austin asks as we wait for one of the six elevators centered on the fourth floor of the company's home office building.

I take in Austin's caramel eyes. "I'd be honored," I say. "Ryan would be honored."

Austin, Marla, and I have three field trips planned a week apart to visit each of our sons' gravesites. Today is Ryan's turn. We all leave something special at each site. A stone. A leaded glass-encased photo. Austin leaves his song.

The whistling in the background grows louder as someone approaches. It echoes in the grand central hall of the building, designed more for opulence than economy. I know who it is before he turns left from the main hallway into the elevator bank where Marla, Austin, and I are standing. Someone I've known for nearly two decades. A former supervisor. When he sees us, he halts. The whistling stops. He throws an arm into the air and snaps his fingers as if he's forgotten something. Then he turns and walks away.

I am familiar with this reaction now. Who wants to share an elevator ride with a grief-stricken parent? A forced moment of intimacy. What to say? We know, especially in these numbers, that we represent unbearable loss. Yet his retreat leaves us silent. A layer of hurt and alienation innocently tossed on top of the trauma. We are to be avoided at all costs. We are what everyone hopes not to be.

What most people don't realize is there is an alarming number of us. We find each other somehow and form a community invisible to most people. Many of us would never otherwise have met. We come from all backgrounds—rich and poor, well-educated and less. We are of diverse religions, cultures and social groups. And we become the closest of friends, glued together by the common experience and understanding of deep grief.

A certain look, and we know one of ours is having a bad day, so we comfort. A certain unintended hurtful word, or the sound of a once special song or the coming across of a specific date. We understand how painful these things are and we reach out to one another with knowing compassion. If in public, it is often only the eyes that speak. *I know. I am here for you.*

Sometimes we say things no parent should ever say. Like, "I wish Ryan had died instantly." I do not have to explain that it destroys me to wonder what he was conscious of in those final hours. The pain he felt. If he fought to say a few last words. We compare types of death. Anticipated versus unanticipated. A long illness versus sudden death. We weigh the benefits and detriments of both.

Other times we laugh at things only we can laugh at. On our visit to Adrian's grave, Austin took in the surroundings, mature landscaping, a gently sloping hill, and said, "I love where Adrian is. It's so beautiful." Of course, Austin wishes Adrian was anywhere else but lying in that cemetery. But we understood, and we chuckled at the incongruity of it.

Now, in the wake left by our whistling colleague, we glance at each other with uncertainty and concern. Here we are, the blond, the black, and the brunette. The Agnostic, the Baptist, and the Jew. No three people can be any closer.

Suddenly, we are laughing, spontaneous and hearty, bent in half, hands to our mouths, trying to muffle the roar. In these numbers, it doesn't hurt so much. In fact, it's downright hilarious. We can't stop laughing.

The Avoidables—stronger somehow in numbers.

A CROSS TOO HARD TO BEAR

The dozen white roses I bought for my father lay in the front passenger seat looking forlorn. We've both been in the heat of the parked car for too long now. I am not sure I have what it takes, even with the roses and every good intention. Even on my father's anniversary.

No matter how I plot the course to my father's gravesite, it takes me past The Cross. The cemetery three miles south of Killer Curve. There is no avoiding it.

When the kids were younger, I took them to the cemeteries to show them where their ancestors were interred. I'd pile them into the car, Amber, Ryan, and the cousins, sometimes with the promise of something special that they called a bribe. "Who wants pizza?" And we'd take a road trip to a cemetery. "This is your great, great grandfather," I told them. Or, "This is your fourth great grandmother." I shared with them what I knew of their ancestor's lives. We pulled weeds and planted flowers. I stressed to them it was important to remember.

We went to my father's grave on occasion, in all innocence traversing Killer Curve, passing the future home of The Cross to get to and from. "This is your grandfather," I told Amber and Ryan. "Remember this cemetery," I urged them.

A drop of perspiration rolls down the left side of my face, bringing me back to the present. *Damn, it's hot.* "Stop capitulating," I say aloud, reaching for a napkin in the center console to wipe my face. "Do something."

After a moment, I start the car with renewed purpose, turn the air on full blast and take a right turn out of the driveway. Destination: cemetery. I don't look to the left or right, but straight ahead, seeing only the goal in my mind's eye. The journey is a blur of time. A struggle to hold back tears.

At the cemetery, I lift the flowers from the front seat beside me, supporting their droopy heads as I would a newborn child. I hold them in a close embrace as I make my way to the grave. Then I gently place the roses intended for my father on the ground above where Ryan lies.

"I'm sorry, dad."

WEDDING

I made it through, I think, congratulating myself. The wedding is over. No one knows the effort it took to attend, entering a church for the first time since Ryan's funeral. On a Saturday. Ryan's thirty-nine-week anniversary. The day before his nine-month anniversary. Eight months and thirty days since Ryan was killed. Two hundred and seventy-three days. But how could we decline the invitation to Bart and Jennifer's wedding?

Shuffling from the sanctuary of the church with Amber and the rest of the crowd toward the receiving line, I realize I don't remember much of the ceremony. It took all my energy to keep my emotions in check. Capturing each wave before it forced an exit, turning it into something resembling a deep catching of the breath. I do recall they prayed to bless the loved ones who died in the past year. *Did they do that for us?* I wonder. I think they probably did. A surge of appreciation overcomes me.

But I remember little else. *God, I wish Michael was with me,* I think as I approach the family. *He's so much better at this.* I seem always to be reeling from the trauma of one thing or another. Like attending a ceremony I fully expected to share with my son. Knowing we will never have this now. Like entering a church again for the first time since Ryan's funeral. Like realizing weddings and funerals are so similar. Friends and family. Ritual. Song and prayer. Like reliving the ceremony that closed the door on my son's life.

They are the same, I would tell Michael if he were with me now. *Weddings and funerals.* And he would understand.

Michael would hold my hand or drape his arm around my waist and buoy me up and say all the words that needed to be said to others so I could gather myself. But Michael is an usher in the wedding. So Amber and I take our positions in single file to greet the lucky couple, their families, and the wedding party.

"Thank you so much for coming." The words startle me even as I step forward into the receiving line. I clasp a hand, force a smile. "I am so happy for you. Such a beautiful ceremony. Just lovely. Congratulations." I make my way down the line, moving like a factory conveyor belt from one person to the next. Trying to get out. "So happy . . . beautiful . . . lovely . . . congratulations . . ." Clasping and hugging and smiling my way from the sanctuary, through the foyer area, to the open doors at the end.

To salvation. To deliverance.

In the opposite direction most people would travel to seek such things.

RECEPTION

Okay, the hard part is over. I sigh to myself, observing the layout of the wedding reception hall while sitting at one of the tables clustered around the dance floor. They thought this through, assigning Amber and me to a dining table near the table of honor, surrounded by our volleyball friends. There will be no awkward small talk. No seemingly innocent questions too difficult to answer. *Do you have children? How many?*

The wedding party enters and the music of the first dance begins. *They are striking together, the newly wed, all aglow. So trusting. Unaware it all can be snatched from them in an instant.* I catch myself. *Stop thinking like that,* I admonish. *Be happy for them.*

The first dance ends and new music fills the hall. The dread descends as the bride dances with her father. This used to be the hardest dance for me. The special dance between father and daughter. A child's ache and longing for a father gone. But it's the realization of what comes next that pits my stomach with fear.

"Isn't she beautiful?" Someone says.

"Lovely," I respond without thinking. "Just lovely." Conditioned now like one of Pavlov's dogs.

I am trapped. The table that set me at ease just moments ago is one of the furthest from the exit. There is no way to escape unnoticed. The groom takes his mother's arm then holds her close and away in the long smooth steps of a waltz.

Oh, Ryan. A loud aching cry escapes. *This is the dance we would have danced.* My yearning for Ryan grows desperate and despite herculean efforts, I cannot stifle the sounds of a mother's grief.

Suddenly Michael is by my side, he urges me onto my feet and walks me the length of the room, through the crowd of tables, toward the front door. I hear my own raw wails reverberating through the hall, forcing their way through my hands that cover my bowed face. Amber follows behind us, someone else follows her. I am sorry. I am so sorry. Yet powerless to stop.

WALKING LIFE'S PERIMETER

"The milk has spoiled again," Michael complains as I walk into the kitchen to find him pouring the last of the gallon down the sink. I try to suppress my irritation. For months now, he has grumbled about spoiling milk. *How trivial,* I think, refraining from saying it aloud. *The milk has spoiled. So what? Ryan is dead.* I relate everything to the fact that Ryan is dead.

"I'll run to the grocery store," I say with seeming charity. My frustration makes me restless. "We need a few things for dinner anyway." Michael gives me a quizzical look. He knows how difficult grocery shopping is for me now. I sense he is about to say something and turn away before he has a chance to speak.

It is Saturday morning and the anniversary of Ryan's death. Just like every Saturday. And just like the seventh day of every month. *Forty-one weeks,* I tell myself as I turn from the driveway onto Main Street. *Nine months and thirteen days since I last saw my son.* I count time in a way I never did before. *Two hundred and eighty-seven days.*

Otherwise, it is a beautiful September morning—blue sky, wispy clouds, a slight comfortable breeze. A welcome break from the August humidity. *Ryan loved days like this. The change of seasons. He would have awoken to the songbirds. He would have . . .* A yearning so great it hurts threatens to overwhelm me and I choke back a sob. I will myself to stop reflecting on things that Ryan loved, what he would have done on a day like today. *I am practiced at this now,* I acknowledge to myself as I turn on the radio to empty my head of thoughts and fill it with NPR chatter. Talk radio, the only radio I can listen to now.

The parking lot is crowded. I prepare myself as I search for a vacant space. *Milk, fruit, veggies, maybe a steak or some chicken for the grill.* I plot out the route. *I'll go down the fruit and vegetable aisle on the far right, follow that to the meat section along the back wall, and then to the dairy section on the left. Good. I can walk the perimeter.*

This won't be so hard. There will be no canvassing the interior aisles past all the labeled foods that Ryan loved. No squeezing my eyes tight as I try to ignore the Juicy Juice and Cheerios and Triscuits. The things I bought just for him. No greeting card aisle with sweet birthday wishes from mother to son and son to mother. Nope, this will be strictly a generic shopping trip—fruit, salad stuff, meat, dairy. I begin to relax.

Following the plan, I snatch up a handbasket as I enter the store and head directly for the aisle on the right. Mango, kiwi, spinach, cucumber, tomatoes. I traipse toward the back, grabbing this and that until I come upon the seafood counter. *Ryan's last meal,* I think as I glance at the lobsters, then quickly away. *Don't,* I scold myself. I turn left, away from the fish tank, and throw a steak into the basket because that is what I see first. Then on to dairy for the milk.

I feel lighter now as I approach the refrigerated case. *Last stop,* I tell myself, pausing to let another shopper make her selection. My shopping basket is nearly full. *Shoot.* I'll have to empty the basket of the fragile items to set the milk on the bottom. *I should have made this the first stop,* I admonish again, looking through the glass case at the milk options. The smaller cartons are at eye level. The gallons of milk are shelved below. I grab the handle and open the door to the cooler.

The thought strikes as I bend down to reach for one of the gallons, immobilizing me. I am frozen in place with the shopping basket in my left hand and my right reaching for that gallon, even as I realize other shoppers are making a wide berth around me.

Someone seizes the door. "Excuse me," he says, opening it wider to release me. I bow my head, set the food basket on the floor, and aim for the exit. I need to get out of here.

By the time I get home and walk through the front door, I am reduced to an exhausted hiccup. It's as if Michael is waiting for me, anticipating this. He doesn't ask what's wrong; just comes up to me and cradles my cheeks in his hands, turning my face up to his. I see pain and questioning in his eyes before he kisses my forehead and pulls me close. I bury my face in his neck and breathe in his scent, the closest thing that comes to consolation.

Michael holds me as I try to catch my breath. "Shhh," he says. "It's okay." The same words he uses to pull me from the nightmares. "It's okay."

He says this even though we both know it isn't.

"I know . . ." Hiccup. "I know why," I tell him in bits and pieces because the words won't roll out of my mouth smooth and polished. They keep clawing their way back to hide in my throat. Maybe we won't have to face the truth if the words can't escape.

"I know why the milk keeps spoiling." Hiccup.

"We're still buying milk for Ryan."

I WRITE

I write. After Michael says goodnight with a tender kiss, and maybe a statement uttered more like a question. "See you soon?" After he grabs whatever book he is reading and mounts the stairs. After I hear the bedroom door close. I write.

I know I should join him, try to ease his loneliness for the woman I was less than a year ago, but I can't. To comfort him would be too much like taking comfort myself, and I've given up on pleasure. The Guilt, capital G, always intrudes, walks in the door, grabs a chair and settles in. The companion I cannot shed.

So I write. To Ryan, for Ryan. Still doing things for my son, as mothers do. Capital G leaves me alone then. When I'm not taking a bite of food that Ryan would have enjoyed. When I'm not appreciating a perfect fall day. When I'm not seeking solace in my husband's embrace.

I write.

NUMBERS

You should have done this before now, I reprimand myself, bending over Ryan's grave to trim the plantings that have gone by. The wind bites at my body through my clothes.

"Four days," I say aloud, clipping the brown leaves of the asters, the leggy catmint, what remains of the coreopsis. There is no one around to hear me.

"Four days until Your Day," I say, using our family's familiar term for birthdays, accentuating the person and the day. Amber's Day. Ryan's Day. Your Day. Our Day. In my mind, I calculate the hours—*twenty-four x three + . . .* I get hung up on whether to count the time leading up to Ryan's Day or the hour of his birth.

I'm a counter now. The anniversaries that make up the days then weeks then months since Ryan's death—*exactly forty-nine weeks; eleven months and eight days; three hundred forty-three days.* The days leading to Ryan's Day—*four days.* Those leading to the anniversary of his death—*twenty-three days.* Me, who never had much of an interest in figures, now tracking all these numbers.

I stuff the plant debris into the plastic bag I've brought with me and look around, thinking again what a dumpy little cemetery this is. No water, no trash receptacle. "I'm sorry Ryan." Capital G.

I am sorry I wasn't thinking more clearly when we chose this cemetery, bought this lot. Sorry I didn't order his monument in time to have it in place for his birthday. Sorry he is dead and alone and has to spend his birthday in such a place.

"Why?" I drop to my knees onto the hard, damp ground. "Why?" I plead, flinging the debris bag as hard as I can, helpless and wailing, and then I am on all fours. Like an animal.

"I can't do this, Ryan." There is so much I cannot do. I can't bear it, all the days without him, all Our Days. I can't change it. I can't go on living without both of my children alive and well.

I crawl onto Ryan's grave and stretch out on the casket length of it so that I am lying in the plant stubble directly on top of him, hugging a mound of earth. "Ryan." Exhaustion moves in like a fog cloud until it is as dense as smoke, smothering me almost silent. "Ryan," I utter again, resigned. My resistance to Ryan's death is not strong enough to bring him back.

The scratches on my face caused by the clipped stems burn from the chill. I lay there a while, accepting the discomfort, and then lift myself up again, onto my hands, then my knees, and crawl from Ryan's grave. When I force myself upright, I am careful not to stand on top of him.

The debris bag is halfway across Ryan's section of the cemetery, lodged against someone's headstone. It's lost about half of its contents in its battle with the wind. A trail of plant clippings marks the way. I follow the path of them, calm now, picking up the prunings as I go, as if I had not just moments before been sprawled across Ryan's grave shrieking at the world.

I see myself as an onlooker might. A bedraggled woman, shivering, knees wet-stained from the earth, an aged brown maple leaf stuck in her hair, slowly retrieving the clippings from her son's grave that fell from the debris bag she hurled across the cemetery a few moments ago. As she walks, she wipes the windburn tears from her cheeks and runs a sleeve beneath her nose.

You're nuts, I tell myself, as I brush the maple leaf from my hair.

Grief so resembles insanity.

RYAN'S DAY

The hand on the oversized wall clock counts the seconds. A soldier's march. Each tick of the second hand is another stride drawing me closer to midnight. Sixteen minutes until Ryan's Day will be done. *How is it possible I am a year older this November 18, and Ryan is not? That there is this Day, Ryan's Day, but no Ryan?*

The shower faucet squeaks in the distance, the sound of the water fades to silence. Michael's footsteps lead one another to his side of the bed. Amber and Kalum have gone home. Nova is sprawled on the floor. Nanauk rests her chin on my knee, her eyes turned up to my face. She is the pooch who worries most about me.

When I woke this morning, I kept my eyes closed. To open them felt too much like opening a door; beckoning the Day to come inside, have a cup of tea, stay awhile. But then I thought about Ryan all alone in the cemetery and the nurturing took over. *I have to make sure Ryan's candle is still lit and the planters are still centered perfectly on the columns at the entrance of the cemetery. And then I need to pick up twenty long-stem white roses for Ryan's grave. And I want to spend time with him. Talk to him.*

So he's not lonely. I don't want Ryan to be lonely. Especially on His Day.

I tried to curb thoughts of birthdays past. Like the last birthday of Ryan's life when he said he was going to invite someone special over for dinner sometime soon. Like Ryan's sixteenth birthday when he announced to all his friends sitting around the table at Chuck's restaurant that he planned to celebrate his twenty-first birthday with his mom.

I tried to avoid thinking that under normal circumstances I would buy him a cookie crumble ice cream cake because he doesn't really care for a baked cake. That for years he pretended to love all those birthday cakes I baked for him in the shape of a heart. And that it took me too long to realize he was just being nice to me. But all the memories came rushing in.

"Oh no." It hits me like a swift uppercut to the jaw and I can't help the corresponding snap of my head. Nanauk startles. "I forgot to get Amber a consolation gift," I explain to the dog. Every year the kid whose Day it isn't gets a consolation gift. It's a family tradition. *But what if there's only one child left? One that can't be consoled?*

This is how family traditions die. Even this small thing feels immensely tragic. *Breathe in, in, in. Breathe out. Slowly now.*

"But overall it was a good day. For what it was. Wasn't it, Nanauk?" Nova looks up at me. "Wasn't it, Nova?"

I went to the cemetery for a total of five times. Once with Michael to lay the white roses. Once with Amber and Kalum and Michael. A third time after dinner with Amber and Kalum and Michael and Pat and Melissa. And twice on my own.

Ryan, your friends stopped by the cemetery all day. Twice while we were there, and twice when we arrived they were already there. Some of them left things for you. And when we all went to the cemetery that final time, we found Chris sitting in the dark by himself. You are loved. You are not forgotten.

Michael and I brought Kalum home with us after the last visit so the kids could have some private time. When Amber came for Kalum, she said lots of people continued to gather at Ryan's gravesite.

The heartbeat of the clock's second hand announces its approach to midnight. The Day did dawn. The Day that Ryan should have celebrated his twentieth birthday. It lounged on the sofa and stayed awhile. It ticked and it tocked. Now I can't wait to boot it out the door.

TERROR IN THE NIGHT

The nightmares haven't left me, even though Michael assured me he'd had that conversation with Bart. That Ryan did have his legs with him in that casket.

"Attached, right?" I had asked.

"Yes," Michael said. "He didn't lose his legs. They were attached to his body."

So now I rarely search for Ryan's legs in my dreams, although I still secretly wonder. The one truth I know is Michael will say just about anything to protect me from the horror of those nightly visions, that fruitless search.

In the new recurring dream, I am behind the wheel of a car traveling far too fast. I am in the driver's seat and the only thing I have control of is the steering wheel. I can turn, but I don't know which way to turn. The car is going too fast and I can't see the barriers ahead. I can't slow down and I can't stop. My legs don't work and I am out of control. I frantically turn the wheel to the left then to the right, trying to maneuver between obstacles I know are there, but I cannot see. I reach a crescendo of fear, realizing I am going to crash. The time that follows is incredibly slow and excruciating. I dream in painful detail what it is like to anticipate the crash and then, immediately before it happens, I awaken, terrified, drenched in sweat. Again and again, this dream marks the start of my day. My inner alarm clock, experiencing what Ryan felt—his fear, his lack of control, his anticipation of death.

I don't know the details of the crash that killed Ryan. What I do know is that The Driver walked away and Ryan never walked again.

WORDS

Last April, Austin asked me if I thought we would have Ryan's monument ready for Memorial Day. *Memorial Day?* I hadn't even thought of it, so worried was I about more temporary things, like candle flames and flowers and angel ornaments that topple to the ground and lose their wings.

"I guess we need to think about getting Ryan a headstone," I suggested to Michael that evening.

"I was wondering when you'd be ready for that," Michael said.

"I don't know if I *am* ready." I was butting heads with my own words. "But we should start thinking about it." A headstone seemed so permanent. Almost like an admission. *I know you are never coming back, Ryan. Ever.* This at a time when I was doing everything in my power to carry him into the future.

But we did start thinking about what would permanently mark Ryan's grave. Once Memorial Day came and went, we decided we would try to have the monument installed for Ryan's Day. If we couldn't do that, we would shoot for his anniversary, December 7. Michael called a local monument company. I designed the stone—six feet tall, polished granite with a saddle-shaped crown. Carved into the saddle at the top will be the head of an angel framed with angel wings. The angel will look down upon Ryan's face, etched in black marble. Beneath that, Ryan's name and dates. As the last phase of the design, we are trying to form the words of a poem that will be etched below his dates. Words that will convey how significant and deeply cherished Ryan is. How essential to our lives.

"The words aren't right," I complain to Michael. "They're not perfect."

"It's a good start," he responds.

I've been dissatisfied with words lately. There aren't enough of them or I cannot combine them in the right way. I feel like I'm letting Ryan down. I have to make up for the unimaginative paragraph of facts in his obituary. "Ryan A. Ramirez, age 19, loving son . . . born in . . . worked as . . . died at . . ."

But I haven't been able to find my voice.

PREPARING FOR THE MONUMENT

I pull the car up behind the white box truck parked at the side of the roadway in front of Ryan's grave and try to swallow the hammering fear in my chest.

"What are you doing?" I ask the two men who are maneuvering a piece of plywood into place where the Christmas tree once stood. They have moved the Christmas tree off to the side.

I left work at two o'clock and headed straight for the cemetery as I do every workday, to relight or replace the candle, check for fallen angels, talk to Ryan and ease his loneliness. It's a shock to see these men molesting this small bit of land I visit every day and so carefully tend.

"We poured the base for the monument," the older man standing directly above Ryan's chest says. Even I am careful never to step on Ryan. I planted dense flowers the long length of his grave so that no one else would.

"You're standing on him," I say. This is why I want a border. To keep people from walking all over Ryan.

"What?"

"Ryan. My son. You're standing on him."

The man steps aside. "I'm sorry ma'am."

"Why didn't anyone tell me you'd be doing this today?" I

glare at one man, then the other. The quiet younger one looks at the older one. He's not about to engage with this distraught woman who might be the same age as his mom.

"We were told to put it in today." The older man shrugs. "So it will cure in time. That's all I know."

"Everything's been approved then?"

"Yeaup."

"Even the granite border?"

"Ayuh."

"Okay, then." The relief of having the border approved appeases me somewhat. "Are you done?"

"Yup. We'll be goin' now." They get into the truck with more haste than they would normally, I suspect. Happy to be distancing themselves from the emotional wreck who has accosted them when they are just doing the job someone hired them to do.

There is a fallen, broken angel lying beneath the Christmas tree. I walk over and pick up it, put it into my coat pocket for mending. When I am sure the truck is gone, I heave aside the plywood board covering the cement footing they poured. The cement looks damp. I touch my index finger to it and discover it is still wet and pliable enough for me to carve words in it. I use my finger to write, "I miss you."

I want to write more. I want to write, "I miss you desperately Ryan, and I love you with all my heart forever how much big is the sky." But the cement is too fluid on the right side of the footing and it won't accept my letters. Even so, I am pleased to have left that permanent expression of my love.

THE MONUMENT

They are still at the cemetery, placing the monument just right. Michael, Amber and I stand in front of it and gaze, speechless. It is a large and weighty stone. This stone we have worked so hard to conceive, this stone we knew until now only in terms of inches and feet and words of gray.

The owner of the monument company called me at work earlier in the day to tell me Ryan's headstone would be delivered just in time. It wasn't ready in time for Ryan's Day, so we were hoping with an inflated sense of desperation it would be in place for December 7.

I wasn't able to leave work immediately, though that was my instinct, always weighing the significance of a thing against the debt I owe my family. Including Ryan in death. What is more important? The scales tipped in only one direction.

I was both excited and anxious. An unsettling fear flutter took residence in my core, stayed with me all the long day, warned me there might be a problem.

But the monument is in its place now. Six feet of Barre granite, with a carved angel protectively overlooking Ryan's etched face, name and dates, a poem of longing beneath that. *Okay, this is a good monument*, I think.

"It's nice," I say aloud. "Majestic."

"Yes," everyone agrees. I wonder if their thoughts follow mine to the insanity of this moment. Admiring a headstone that symbolizes the death of someone we love with such force. The missing piece of the puzzle of our family. Incomplete now.

But it is a majestic monument and everyone who sees it will know how much Ryan is loved. *Ryan, you would like this,* I whisper. I feel almost happy.

~

WE DON'T KNOW what to do with ourselves, so we go to the cemetery to take another look at the monument. We stand staring at it in all its glory, memorizing every little detail.

When I spot it, I almost don't believe it, shut my eyes tight and open them again.

"Oh, my God."

"What?" Michael asks. My stomach is in my throat.

"What?" Michael says, more insistent.

I am stunned, like someone walloped me across the side of the head. Such an important and significant thing, the thing I was terrified would not turn out just right, didn't. All that time and attention to it. Picking the stone. It had to be larger than life. Designing the angel. Deciding on the contrast between the polished and rough-hewn parts. Writing the poem. Checking the commas to be sure they were all in the right places. Reviewing it time and again.

"Oh, my God," I say again. "Read it. Read the poem."

Michael reads aloud as I continue to stare at the omission.

> "Here lies a son, a brother,
> an uncle, a cousin, a friend;
> a life full of promise
> too early to end.
> So deeply mourned,

> he lies not alone,
> his future lies with him,
> his children unborn.
> He lies with his dreams,
> unrealized, unspoken
> he rest . . ."

Michael pauses a moment, and I know he's spotted the last missing "s" in the word that should have read "rests." Then he continues to read as if the letter isn't missing.

> ". . . he rests in our hearts,
> forevermore broken."

"I can't believe it," he says. "We reviewed everything so carefully." He turns to me and asks, "Whose mistake was it?"

I stand silent, biting my lower lip. *I'm sorry Ryan. I am so sorry. I wanted everything to be perfect for you.*

COUNT DOWN

"Sher," Michael shouts from downstairs. I turn my back to the snowflakes falling outside the bedroom window and grab my jacket from the foot of the bed. "Are you ready?" His footsteps trail his voice up the stairs.

"Yeah." It comes out too low. "Yes," I say with more power so my voice will carry through the open bedroom door to the left and left again, halfway down the stairs. Even the bit of extra air I have to expunge to speak at an above-normal tone, the added force required of my diaphragm, seems too much.

I wait the few seconds he takes to reach the bedroom doorway before asking, "Do you have everything?"

"In the car," Michael says. "The sheet, the ribbon, the snow shovel."

"The candle?"

"Yes. That too. The car's warmed up. Amber and Kalum are waiting."

It is storming just like it was a year ago and I feel a drumbeat of dread as the moments bring me closer to the time Ryan died. It is the day before the one-year anniversary of his death. The last day of the last month in which I can tell myself, *Ryan was still alive a year ago.*

~

Michael shovels a short path to the monument and then a narrow area around both it and the decorated white pine that stands to the left of it. I look for flying angels in the snow he tosses when he's nearest the tree, amazed that they all seem to have stayed intact. The star on top keeps watch over the angels that adorn the tree below it. That dance in the wind below it. That sometimes crash to the ground below it. When Michael finishes shoveling, I remove an angel I've glued back to life from my coat pocket and place it deep inside a branch to protect it from further damage. That dastardly wind.

Michael and I battle with gusts of cold air to dress Ryan's monument with the crisp white sheet and secure it with a long strip of lace in preparation of the unveiling ceremony scheduled for tomorrow. We are careful not to step on the grave itself. The Christmas tree is an obstacle. It's a little tricky, but we manage to get it done. I step back from the stone monolith to gaze at it. Amber stands bundled but shivering in the plowed roadway holding Kalum's gloved hand. Kalum, in his brilliant yellow snow jacket, is a spot of color in the gray landscape. He wants to play in the snow. Michael grabs the snow shovel and clears a larger area surrounding Ryan's monument.

"Kalum," Michael says, "help me shovel."

"Okay!" Kalum pulls himself from Amber's grasp to go help Grandpa. His giggle brings me back to a year ago when I last heard Ryan's laugh through the phone line. *The first anniversary of the last time I heard Ryan laugh.* I close my eyes and try not to let the memory pierce my heart, then raise my head and force myself to focus again on the draped monument.

"This is good I think." Everyone leaves it to me to say what is acceptable when it comes to Ryan. Michael leans on the snow shovel and nods. Amber gazes at the covered stone. Even Kalum stops to look. No one says anything.

The sheet adorning Ryan's gravestone is a few shades less brilliant than the fresh, untouched snow surrounding the shoveled area. Its fabric is belted in the middle with the white lace whose daintiness belies its strength. The skirt below the belt whips in the wind like a woman dancing tango in a monochrome world, revealing glimpses of the secrets that lie beneath. Peeks at words of unfathomable loss and longing. A hint of a letter omitted.

You can't help but look.

ANNIVERSARY

I catch the full length of myself in the bedroom mirror. *A year.* I can't believe it's been a year. *I've lived a year without Ryan. My son.* Without seeing Ryan's square jawline, or the curve of his smile, or the laughter in his almond-shaped eyes. Without touching Ryan's arm, or brushing my hand through his hair, or running my nails down his spine. Without hearing Ryan speak. My heart surges with longing to hear another, "I love you, mom." The words he often said instead of goodbye, shouting them out through a crowd of his teenage friends. Do I remember Ryan's voice? Yes, I can still hear his voice.

How are you? I mouth to my reflection. It doesn't respond. Doesn't have to. I see the woman in the mirror has journeyed far in the past year. Her face is drawn and pale. Her hair has lost its luster. Her clothes don't fit anymore. I want to tell her that she really should replace her wardrobe. But I can see clothes don't matter to her anymore. She doesn't have the energy for such menial tasks. It's all she can do to get out of bed in the morning. She forgets appointments. She drops things. Her mind cannot concentrate the way it used to.

Michael walks into the bedroom and stops to assess the same reflection. "How are you?" he asks. Still no response. I feel removed from the woman in the mirror. She'll have to answer on her own.

"Did you talk to the plow guy?" I ask.

"Yes. He said he'd get it done. He knows everyone's meeting here at eleven."

"But does he know how many people are coming?" I am worried something will go wrong. "That he has to plow—"

"Yes," Michael interrupts. "He knows he has to plow the field. I'm taking care of it. Don't worry, okay?" The shrill of the wind outside fills the few seconds of silence.

"But we can't even get out to see what the cemetery looks like. What if it's not plowed? And we need enough time to shovel it out again."

I feel the weight in Michael's sigh as he turns and walks out of the room.

∽

THE CONVOY to the cemetery reminds me of the procession that followed the hearse a few days short of a year ago. It's not nearly as long though. And this time it's our car leading the way. I try to push a thought from my head. *The crowd is dwindling. From year to year, it will get smaller and smaller until it's just me. Traveling to the cemetery all by myself.* I don't want Ryan to read my mind. It would hurt him to know this. I hum the notion out of my head. "Hmmm . . ." long and flat and soft. A mosquito buzz. Michael turns to glance at me from the driver's seat. He doesn't say anything. Neither does Amber, who is sitting with Kalum in the back seat. Staring straight ahead I interrupt myself only to take a breath. I exhale another "Hmmm . . ."

The caravan follows as we make the left turn from Main Street onto the unnamed road leading to the cemetery and the sewer plant. Even though Michael made this trip earlier to confirm the cemetery was plowed, and he again shoveled the area surrounding Ryan's grave, the worry doesn't completely release me until I see it for myself.

"It's pretty."

"Yeah," Amber agrees.

"Hmm," Michael acknowledges, mimicking my earlier hum. I turn to look at him, wondering if he's making an attempt at humor. *Hey, that's my line*, I want to say. If we were in another time and place, I would say it aloud. In another time and place, we would have appreciated the quip. We would have chuckled. But now Ryan is dead and there is no room for lightheartedness. He doesn't return my gaze so I turn my attention back to the landscape.

It's a picture of muted contrast. The snow, fresh and pristine. The pine trees in the background almost black, juxtaposed with the bright white. The heads of stones stand in perfect alignment, proud and straight, a darker gray than the sky. Ryan's monument, though daintily dressed and sashaying at the waist, stands tallest and proudest of them all. It stunts the Christmas tree to the left of it, where even the color of the angel ornaments is muted. Wisps of snow leap from the ground to romp in the wind.

Once Michael sees that all the vehicles behind us have made it through the cemetery entrance, he parks the Nissan on the side of the roadway just beyond Ryan's grave.

I grapple with the wind to open the passenger-side door. The battle is won, but not without punishment. One gust gives me a sharp slap in the face. "Wow." I bow my head and tell Kalum, who is sitting behind me, "Get out on your mom's side."

"Let me out," he says to Amber.

Vern and Jen emerge from the vehicle behind us, bundled in snow jackets. Pat and Melissa follow, along with the other Melissa and Dan and Chris and the other Dave and Danyelle and Chelsea and Julianna and Justin and Kellie and Mike and Nancy and Vivian and Roxanne and the rest of them. They all battle with the squalls to make their way to Ryan's monument.

Most carry with them an angel ornament. Some bring flowers. One girl holds the ribbon of an oversized gold metallic balloon with a smiley face on it. I want to turn it on its head, cause the smile to become a frown. There is nothing happy about today.

The wind roughs us up as Amber addresses the crowd, saying words I cannot hear through the whistle of the squalls charging past my ears. My hair whips my cheeks. I wonder if it is Ryan making all this ruckus, so upset at being dead now. Melissa speaks after Amber, her words lost as well. I resign myself to it. So much has been lost.

I untie the piece of lace holding the sheet in place on Ryan's monument. Michael and Amber remove the veil as everyone watches. People ooh and aah. They place angels on Ryan's Christmas tree. Kalum makes angels with his body in the snow. I try not to let my eyes fall on the omitted letter.

All day, I have relived that other day one year ago, acknowledging each anniversary within the anniversary. 4:12 A.M., The Phone Call. 4:59 A.M., pacing in a waiting area in the hospital begging God to let Ryan live. 6:00 A.M., the moment Ryan died. 6:10 A.M., hearing the words, "I'm sorry," from the trauma surgeon.

I cannot help but think that one year ago today we were sitting with the funeral director right about now.

PART III
PURPOSE AND FRENZY

In Memoriam

Ryan,
I say your name now
as often as I ever did.

Walking down hallways,
driving down highways,
I call your name,
whisper your name,
I cry your name.

So afraid of losing that too,
the familiarity of your name.

PURPOSE BORN

It was the photo in the newspaper that first caught my eye. Grieving parents standing in front of the tree that stopped the car that killed their sixteen-year-old son. Then the date struck me. *Oh, just ten days after Ryan,* I thought. At the same time, the name of the town in which the crash occurred registered with me. *And right next door.*

Danny's crash occurred on December 6, the crash that killed Ryan happened on December 7, and then this one that killed Joey on December 17. I do the math. Within eleven days, and about a twenty-five-mile radius, five teenagers and a young father of three were killed in crashes involving three different teen drivers. Others were injured. Kids and cars and crashes. *It's an epidemic.* The revelation astounded me. *Kids are killing themselves and other kids at an alarming rate.*

I read through the article. There is going be a presentation on teen driving safety at a local high school. This family will take part. I know I have to be there.

"Janice!" I spot her almost instantly upon entering the auditorium. Janice, who I know from Compassionate Friends. Janice, whose son Dan was killed just six hours prior to the crash that took Ryan's life one town away. Janice, whose son's crash I had used in my calculations to realize we have a crisis on our hands. Here we are, both attending this assembly on safe teen driving in a crowded high school auditorium, preparing to listen to local politicians and that family whose photo I saw in the newspaper. Evidently, Janice had seen the article too.

Janice is as startled to see me as I am to see her. We hug and settle side-by-side into our seats. We learn from one senator about the importance of graduated driver licensing, known as GDL, laws and listen as the mom, Connie, talks about her beloved son Joey. Following the presentation, we meet with them all and it is clear what we have to do. We have to educate ourselves, and then others. We have to put an end to this needless and preventable devastation.

LONGING

*M*ichael closes the mouth of the book he's been reading at the same time he winds-up a yawn. "It's late," he says, lifting himself from the love seat. "I'm going to go take a shower." He kisses the top of my head.

"Okay, I'm right behind you," I lie before turning back to the television. Trying to hide the relief I feel that I will have some time alone to grieve. *My grief evenings.* I have to protect the living from the ugliest of it—the open and raw expression of intolerable anguish and longing. And I have to talk to Ryan. Or write to him. This is our time, late at night.

Michael pauses at the foot of the stairway and we study one another for a prolonged moment. The hurt, the longing, the questions on his face stab at my heart. He wants the old me back. But there is no room to pile all his pain onto my own, so I lower my eyes and again pretend to focus on the newscast. It is another moment longer before I hear him make his way up to the bedroom. *I'm sorry, Michael.*

"I'm so sorry," I exhale in a whisper. But now I am talking to Ryan. "For everything that was taken from you." *He so desperately wanted to live.* "Your wife and children." *He wanted to have three children.* Tears carve down my face. I know they will leave a mark on the landscape, as a river channeling through a mountain pass does. *His progeny.* I double over, dropping my face to my knees. *So many futures wiped out.* "I, I'm sorry you'll never wake up to the songbirds again," I stutter. "That you'll never wake up again at all." My breathing is staccato, in three times, then out, quick and sharp. It has its own primitive rhythm. "I miss you so much, Ryan. I don't know how to live without you." I moan and whisper Ryan's name, beg for "Ryaaan, Ryyyan, Ryaaan," breaking into a new torrent of quiet sobs. "I will never stop saying your name, Ryan," I promise in my one-sided conversation with him. I've learned to control the volume of this nightly ritual so as not to disturb the living, but I cannot control the sheer force of it.

CHRISTMAS

"Not bad," I step back to gaze at the live Norfolk pine that a group of friends gave us after Ryan died. It's about a foot taller than I am. We've waited until this Christmas day to string it with white fairy lights and place a star at the top before Amber and Kalum arrive. We cannot stomach looking through the family Christmas boxes for decorations, so it will be a non-traditional, low-key Christmas. The second Christmas without Ryan.

Michael and I have already been to the cemetery. The tree next to Ryan's monument is more ornate than the Norfolk at home. But they both sport a carbon copy of the same star on top.

"It's fine," Michael agrees, stepping forward to adjust the silver metal star again. It keeps tilting to the right. *Just like Ryan*, I can't help but think. How I raised a kid who leaned to the conservative is beyond me. I shake the thought from my head.

"The turkey smells good," I offer.

"Thanks. I hope they get—"

Nanauk barks. Nova's tail wags. The dogs charge from where we are standing in the living room to the front door right before it opens.

"Hi," Amber greets the dogs.

"Hi!" Kalum hollers. "We're here!" The hollering and sounds of wagging tails smacking against the wall and snow boots stomping on the entry rug remind me of how quiet the house is now.

"Why don't you put on some Christmas music?" I ask Michael.

"Perfect timing," Michael shouts over his shoulder and the havoc to Amber and Kalum as he heads to the stereo. "Linner's just about ready." It startles me that he uses our family's made-up word for a cross between "lunch" and "dinner," served around two or three in the afternoon and usually reserved for special occasions. The word has a lightness to it. It speaks of family tradition. It doesn't seem to fit.

He's trying, I acknowledge to myself. *Just like me requesting the Christmas music.* I walk toward the front hallway to greet my daughter and grandson. Kalum's father isn't with them. Grief has taken its toll on Amber and Mike's relationship. Perhaps it simply hastened the inevitable. Our poor family has been reduced by a third in just over a year. Yet here we are, a shrunken family of four pretending that the grief hasn't settled in, not fooling anyone, preparing to eat a Christmas linner made for six.

!MPACT

We are fevered, the three families of three boys who died in separate car crashes within eleven days of one another. We hold meetings. We work to form a nonprofit organization. We develop a program for high schools patterned after the program Joey's family delivered.

We adopt my suggestion for a company name and acronym: Mourning Parents Act, Inc., also to be known as !MPACT. We approve Janice's suggestion for a mission: To eliminate tragedies caused by inexperienced drivers through awareness, education, and legislation. In no time at all, Connie, Janice and I are booked for presentations at local high schools. We educate ourselves. We meet with legislators to raise awareness of the dangers of teen driving. We advocate for GDL laws that will introduce young drivers to the driving experience in a gradual manner. We testify before the state legislature. Increase driver training hours, we urge. Limit passengers. Adopt nighttime driving restrictions. Ban electronics.

"I will carry you into the future," I promise Ryan. And I do.

Large posters with our boys' faces accompany us on stage in what would come to be known as our Drive 4 Tomorrow presentations. We show memorial videos. We talk of our love for our children and the details of our very personal experiences of tragedy and loss.

We don't preach. We share.

And the kids listen.

DANGER

Terror strikes when I hear the sirens. They are close and persistent. There are many of them, and they don't travel out of earshot. I listen for clues as each of the sirens come to a stop.

Oh, God. I don't know where Amber and Kalum are. Michael is taking care of some chores at 60, our rental property. As I grab the phone, I try to judge the distance of the unfolding calamity from the house. A half a mile maybe? I fumble with Amber's number. Her phone rings several times, then goes to voice mail. *Please call me as soon as possible Amber. It's important.* I pause a moment before leaving my name and phone number. Not because Amber wouldn't know who it was or how to contact me. But because someone else might get the message. Like an EMT. Or a police officer. That my family is at risk of dying at any moment is all too real to me.

I call Michael's cell phone, grab my purse from the newel post at the base of the stairs and run out the front door to the car. The February chill reprimands me. *You didn't grab a coat*, it chides. *Not important*, I retort. Michael isn't answering either. *Please, God.* I toss the phone to the passenger seat with more force than necessary and drive down our private road to Main

Street. A police car flies by, lights on, wailing like the rest. *He shouldn't be going that fast. That's risky. Very risky.* I take a left onto Main Street to follow at a safe distance. Up ahead I see the police car turn left onto the road leading to 60. *No.* I take the same left. *No. Please. No.* My heart is stomping in my chest. Halfway down the road, a truck with flashing emergency lights straddles the centerline, blocking access from that point on. An older man in a reflective vest who I faintly recognize as a volunteer with the fire department raises his hand to stop me as I approach. Then he circles his pointer finger in the air. *Turn around*, it demands.

"Is it a car crash?" I shout as I lower the car window. He saunters over to the driver's side. "Is it a car crash?" I repeat.

He sees my tears, looks at me with caution, makes some silent decision and nods his head, yes. "A single-vehicle accident."

"Oh, God. What kind of vehicle is it?" He doesn't answer. "Is it a dark blue Volvo?"

"No."

"Is it a white van?"

"No."

"Are you sure? Really sure?" I plead. "You saw it?"

"Yes ma'am, I'm sure. It's not a Volvo, and it's not a van."

"Oh, thank God. Thank you."

There is a wail from behind demanding access.

"You need to turn around," the faintly familiar man says. There is a trail of cars in my rearview mirror. Another police vehicle is trying to squeeze forward. I swing the Xterra to the right, then reverse and forward again in a classic Y turn. *Thank God.* I feel a torrent of relief as I drive home.

DOMINIC

I did all that pleading and gave thanks to a God I'm not sure I believe in because I needed Amber and Kalum and Michael to be okay. And they were. But when Melissa called to tell me it was Dominic in that car, I felt guilty for the pleas and the thanks and the relief. The pleas should have been broader. *Please, God. Let no one have been badly hurt.* The thanks and relief were premature. They aren't compatible with a critically injured Dominic lying in the hospital. Dominic, with the crooked smile who is only seventeen-years-old. Dominic, whose older brother Dan had carried the weight of Ryan in a casket fourteen short months ago. Dominic, who was born on his mother Marjolaine's birthday, just like Ryan was born on mine.

∼

DOMINIC'S DAD Bob cracks the front door to Amber and me, and two large pans of warm lasagna in our arms. A hearty offering for a family who might forget to eat. He opens the door wider to let us in. Marj enters the room and takes the pans from our grasp, one at a time, offering thanks. She disappears into the kitchen twice. The hugs come later.

Marj and Bob share the details, and we try to offer comfort across the dining room table. But the truth is, there is no comfort to give or to be had. That Dominic is gone for good hasn't settled with them yet. Their future without their youngest son looms ahead.

"You can ask for a palm print," I tell them. "A cast of his hand." My gaze is drawn down to my own hands folded in my lap, remembering the devastation I felt when Connie shared that the hospital had offered her a cast of Joey's palm. "I wish I had," I say. "I wish I had known." I am trying to think of anything that might be helpful. "And you can ask for a lock of his hair. I wish I had that too."

I'm thankful now that Amber insisted we come. I feel I'm being useful.

"But what if they don't want company?" I asked her. "I didn't. Remember?" I was concerned we would be more of an intrusion than anything.

"Mom, we have to," she said. So here we are.

"I wondered how you do it," Marj says. "Now I guess I'll find out."

"Have you made arrangements?" I ask because that is the innocuous term you use when speaking of wakes and funeral services and cemeteries and burial.

Marj nods. Her eyes are damp. She sighs. Her pale face, framed by dark chocolate waves, carries the shock and weariness I am so familiar with. The look that still occasionally gazes at me from the bathroom mirror. Marj and Bob give us the dates and times and locations. When one trails off, the other steps in.

"He'll be buried right next to Ryan," Marj adds.

My heart catches in my throat. "*Right* next to Ryan?" *Oh no.* The cemetery sexton had promised to reserve that double lot for us. I'm planning to be next to Ryan, and Michael will be on the other side of me. Our names are already engraved in stone on the back of Ryan's monument.

She nods. "We thought . . . well, we thought when the kids

go to the cemetery, they can visit both of them at the same time."

"Wait. *Right* next to Ryan?" I ask again, incredulous. "Not one lot over, but *right* next to him?" I know I am not being supportive in the least, but I can't help myself. Bob nods. Amber, sitting to my left, glares at me. I can see her in my peripheral vision but refuse to turn her way.

"Did you already buy it?" I try not to act too alarmed despite the probing questions, despite the perspiration emanating from every pore of my face.

"This morning," Bob says.

"I'm sorry, but . . . but that's supposed to be our lot," I blurt. Amber kicks my leg under the table. Though we had reserved the lot next to Ryan, the actual purchase would entail the exchange of two cremation lots we had in another town cemetery. It was going to be a process I hadn't yet found the energy for. "I can't believe he sold it," I add, doing my best to ignore Amber.

"We'll call him," Bob says getting up from the dining chair at the head of the table. "We'll tell him we want to trade it for another one." Marj hands Bob the phone. He pulls a piece of paper out of the pocket of his jeans and dials.

Through the one-sided conversation, I learn the next lot over is available. Bob looks to Marj, who nods. They'll take that one, fix the paperwork later.

Thank God Amber talked me into coming today. I've got to finalize that cemetery transaction.

∼

"Do you have any tissues?" I whisper into Michael's ear. He shakes his head, no. I turn to Amber on the other side of me. "Do you have any tissues?" She looks at me with widening eyes. That would be a no. *How on earth did I forget to bring tissues to Dominic's funeral?*

St. Mary is packed with teenagers. The seating is U-shaped.

Looking around, I see some familiar faces. Many of these same kids were at Ryan's funeral, and Billy's before that. I shake my head to empty it.

My gaze settles on a face directly across the sanctuary and my heart takes a stomach dive. I elbow Amber and Michael on either side of me. "Is that . . .?" I sense the turning of their heads to follow my eyes. Now I am certain of it. The Driver is sitting in nearly our exact location opposite us so we cannot look straight ahead without seeing him, and he, us. No matter how hard we try, we cannot avoid catching each other's eyes. I feel trapped, and focus my attention at the entrance hall to the left as the funeral begins.

It hits especially hard when I see the casket. There is so much tragedy in the world. Billy's gone. Ryan's gone. Danny's gone. Joey's gone. Josh and Adrian are gone. Now Dominic's gone. All these kids shouldn't be attending their friend's funerals. And I shouldn't have to be looking into the eyes of the kid who didn't mean to extinguish my son's life, yet did.

Tears gush down my face. I try to muffle the sounds coming from my throat. I am crying out at injustice. I am crying for all of humanity. I am crying because Ryan and Dominic will lay one plot away from each other in the graveyard.

Dominic, whose mother had promised to write her special memories of Ryan and share them with me. Dominic, whose mother can never bring herself to do that now. Dominic, who will carry that little piece of Ryan to his grave with him.

So much is lost with a life.

TERROR IN A CAR

"Michael, slow down," I tell him, horse hooves cantering in my chest.

"I'm going the speed limit," he responds. When I crane my neck to look at the speedometer, I see he is. Sixty-five miles per hour on the nose.

"Well, don't follow so close behind the vehicle in front of us," I say, clutching the armrest with my right hand, left hand in front of me on the dashboard.

"I've been driving for decades. I know how to drive."

"I can't help it," I say, trying to calm myself. "It's just that," I stop, not knowing how to say it. "It's just that I'm so afraid. I mean really terrified."

"I'm a safe driver Sher," Michael says more tenderly. "Nothing bad is going to happen."

"It's not that I don't trust you. What I don't trust is circumstance," I try to explain. "And sometimes I feel the impact. Ryan's impact. That killed him. With anything abrupt. Like a change in acceleration. Or the pressing of brakes. I know it sounds strange, but I do."

Michael pats my leg but says nothing. I've told him this

much, I might as well tell him the whole of it. Well, almost the whole of it.

"And I feel like I'm going to die in a car crash too."

Michael lets the distance grow between our vehicle and the pickup truck in front of us. "You're not going to die in a car crash," he says.

What I don't share is that this is my new nightmare, the anticipation of the crash and the terror that awakens me. That it leaves me wondering what Ryan's last view of the world was. What is the last thing he saw? What did he experience in his last cognitive moment? Was he in pain? Did he know he was dying? Please, please, let him have been unaware.

CEMETERY COMMISSION

"I make a motion to appoint Sherry Chapman," comes from the television in the background. The Town Council meeting on the local public access channel is airing in another room as we tidy up the kitchen following dinner.

"Michael!" I shout, rushing to stand in front of the television. He walks over to join me.

"They said my name," I tell him, grabbing the remote control and hitting the rewind button.

Yes, I heard it right. "I make a motion to appoint Sherry Chapman to the Cemetery Commission," one Council member says. "I second," says another. "All in favor say aye," the Town Council chairman says. "Aye," the Council members say in unison. "That's unanimous," says the chair. "Motion passes."

Michael and I look at one another incredulous. Then he smiles at me, and I smile back. "Congratulations," he says.

There were so many reasons why we could not bring Ryan home where I wanted him. We would have to establish a cemetery on our property, get a special permit from the Planning and Zoning Commission, purchase surrounding property that was not for sale to have the proper access. One roadblock after another. We finally realized it was not possible. I had promised to bring him home. I can't do that. But I can bring home to him.

I decided I needed to improve and beautify the cemetery he's in, so when I saw there was a vacancy on the Cemetery Commission, I applied. But that was two months ago. And no one had contacted me. I thought they had passed me up. Someone from the Public Works Department might have told them, "She's that crazy woman who came bursting in here sobbing and demanding that we plow the cemeteries." I assumed they were holding out for a more suitable candidate.

I had all but given up hope. But here I am, a newly appointed member of the Cemetery Commission, effective today. My heart begins to sing as my surprise settles.

"You'd think someone would have told me I was still under consideration," I complain to Michael, petulant but self-satisfied.

PREPARING FOR SENTENCING

Almost a year and a half. "Why does it take so long?" I ask, not directing my question to anyone in particular. Amber remains silent in the back seat. Michael lets a moment pass before he responds.

"They probably think it will be less emotional. Less inflamed if they let a certain amount of time pass."

"But it doesn't work that way," I rebut. "It's torture. The continuances. The way they drag it out like this. It's not like there's any question over what happened."

"I know," he says, taking his eyes off the road to risk a glance at me. "But it will soon be over. This part anyway."

"It's another ending," I lament. All these things involving Ryan keep ending. I want it over, but I dread the endings.

"Are you nervous?" Michael asks. He might be referring to my anxiety over the statement I plan to read in court, or over possible press coverage, or the uncertainty of the sentencing. His words invoke a physical response. Suddenly everything is exaggerated; the beat of my heart, the flush of perspiration on my forehead. A response so much like fear. Fight or flight. I want to run away. Instead, I take a long slow breath. Let it out.

"No," I respond.

SENTENCING

The victim's advocate sits to my left in the first row of benches, facing the Superior Court judge. Michael and Amber flank my right. The courtroom is full. Behind us are reporters from the *Hartford Courant*, *The Chronicle*, the *Journal Inquirer*. Behind them our friends Austin, Marla, Janice, others. Our support system. Somewhere to the left of us on the opposite side of the courtroom is the defendant and his family.

It's good they reached a deal. A trial would be worse, I remind myself with a shiver. It's cold. A deep bone cold. I am a lot leaner than I was a year, four months and twenty days ago when Ryan was still alive. Five hundred and seven days ago. Twelve thousand one hundred and sixty-eight hours ago. The chill doesn't meet much resistance before reaching my bones.

I lean over to Michael's ear. "Are you cold?" *No,* he shakes his head imperceptibly.

We listen as the lawyer for The Driver drones on, exercising his right to argue for less. The plea agreement includes incarceration for a set period but allows the defense to make a case that less time should be served. The judge will make the final determination.

The Driver's lawyer sounds like background noise until I

hear him say "Ryan" and I snap to attention. *Did I just hear that?* He says Ryan's name again. I glance at Amber and see her looking at me with a frown between her eyes.

Amber leans her head toward me. "He said Ryan when—" she whispers.

"—when he was referring to The Driver," I finish for her. "What a jerk."

The lawyer does it again, says Ryan's name instead of The Driver's name. *Is he really that confused, or is he doing it on purpose?* I am beginning to wonder.

"Why is he doing that?" I ask Michael after the third time. The lawyer repeatedly refers to his client as Ryan. As if they are interchangeable—my son and this other boy. It is the only thing I hear now. I wait for Ryan's name to come out of his mouth. And it does, again and again. Stabs me in the heart like a dagger. Again, and again.

HAPPY MOTHER'S DAY

It is the Friday before Mother's Day. Janice and I are presenting !MPACT's Drive 4 Tomorrow program at a high school. The auditorium is filled with hundreds of teenagers, stone silent, listening intently to every word as we share our personal stories. It is always like this when we talk. Sober and silent. Janice was first to speak. Now I am telling them about the hospital experience.

"We heard footsteps, and then someone said, 'I'm sorry. He rallied there for a while.' Afterward, all I could think about were those words, 'he rallied there for a while.' I knew that meant Ryan must have fought very, very hard to live." Tears are streaming down my cheeks.

I talk about seeing Ryan in death and meeting with the funeral director.

"What kind of coffin would a teenager like?"

I talk about the autopsy and going through all of Ryan's things, preserving cards and notes and photos never intended for my eyes.

"You have no privacy when you die like Ryan did."

I share how different life is now. Grieving parents can't talk about dead children in most social circles, but here I can talk about Ryan.

"I listen to the wind in a way I never did before, and with a certain gust, I'm off to the cemetery to set things right again."

Following our talks, we show a memorial video of one of the kids. We rotate to be fair because we love showing our kids' memorial videos. Today it's Ryan's turn. The slide presentation shows Ryan growing up, with video clips and still photos. It includes some of the notes he wrote to me. It ends with a scene of the car, The Cross, Ryan's monument, news articles, the sentencing.

A Mother's Day card he once gave me appears on the screen. "I hope you have a very happy Mother's Day. You are the best mother in the whole wide world. Love, your one and only favorite son, Ryan."

It hits me extra hard today and I have to walk out of the auditorium while the video is playing to compose myself. I prepare for the substance of the program that follows. The kids will listen now that they've heard our personal stories and gotten to know us and our sons.

I walk back up to the stage as the video ends. I almost cannot believe I am here, in this place, doing this presentation in front of hundreds. My life is so different now.

"Motor vehicle crashes are the number one killer of teenagers in America," I begin. "If you die young, in all likelihood you will die as the result of a car crash."

I talk about factors and statistics, and they continue to listen. We touch their hearts, and that gives us access to their heads. I'm blunt with them as I speak of the violence of car crashes, what happens to the body, the three impacts. They don't want to die this way. I tell them how they can protect themselves and their friends.

At the end of the presentation, Janice and I stand by the doors as the kids exit. Some of them are crying. "Thank you," one after another says. One boy hugs Janice, then me, and says he's sorry. After that, the hugs become the accepted expression of emotion, and we get one hug after another.

"Please carry this with you. Be safe," we repeat.

"I will. Thank you."

"You opened my eyes."

"You remind me of my mom. I would never want this to happen to her."

"I would hate for something like that to happen to me or my friends."

As the crowd thins, a girl who was standing back waiting for a gap in line walks up to me for a hug. Her eyes are red-rimmed.

"I just want you to know how sorry I am," she says as she reaches out for an embrace. "It broke my heart."

"Thank you. Just make sure you don't place yourself in risky situations."

"I won't," she says as we disengage. "I'm going to tell one of my friends I'm not going to ride with her anymore. She scares me."

"Good," I say. "You need to have that honest conversation with her."

"Well, I hope you have a happy Mother's Day."

I am caught off guard but manage to hold it all in until she walks away. Then I cover my face with my hands.

"Sher?" I feel Janice's touch on my back.

"She wished me a happy Mother's Day," I whisper through the aching that envelops my whole body.

"It broke my heart."

GIRL AT THE CEMETERY

I turn the steering wheel slightly to drive through the puddle at the entrance of the cemetery to leave my mark in the form of tire tracks, however temporary. Proof that someone was here. *See Ryan? You're not forgotten. Look at that damp stretch of a tire track leading right to your grave.*

My heart swells when I spot the girl sitting on the concrete park bench that borders the left side of Ryan's grave, her mid-length coffee-dark hair spilling from her bent head. *Maybe I should just drive by*, I think, *give her more time alone with him.* But I can't, so I creep the Nissan behind her car and sit a moment, appreciating the late-spring sunshine before opening the door and stepping out. She lifts her face to mine.

"Are you Ryan's mom?" she asks. I nod, and she goes on. She credits Ryan for changing her life, she goes to church now, she visits Ryan's grave often and talks to him. I am surprised I haven't run into her before now. She tells me her last name is Ryan.

"I have a photograph of him. His last photograph," she says. "It was taken two days before he . . ." she pauses.

"Two days before?" I ask. My heartbeat goes rapid.

"Yes, I can make you a copy."

There is nothing more that I want right now, nothing within reach anyway, than a copy of that photograph. "Please," I say. "I have a photo I took nine days before he died. I thought that was his last." Then after a pause, "It would mean so much to me to have a copy of that photo. Please."

"Yes," she promises. "If you give me your address, I'll mail it to you." I give her my address. She points out the heart-shaped stone she placed on the foot of Ryan's monument and tells me The Driver is her best friend.

GIRL AT THE RESTAURANT

It was strange from the beginning, standing among the milling crowd of former real estate law colleagues, most of whom I hadn't seen for years, waiting for the hostess to seat us. Me wondering, *How on earth did I think I was up for this?*

My friend Joyce, who drove us here, bounced between old friends. I'm not sure anyone other than Joyce knew about Ryan. Or maybe they did. But no one said anything. In fact, I felt as if I was being avoided but, then again, I was doing plenty of the avoiding myself, eyes darting away if they settled on a glance. *What would I say?* The chatter accosted my ears.

I took a seat in the restaurant's lobby and observed the woman whose name I didn't remember.

She was probably in her mid-sixties now—nonverbal, vacant, frightened—clinging to her husband's arm as he talked with another couple. Her eyes were wide, her lips tight. Her head darted here and there and sometimes settled on her husband's shoulder. I felt oddly connected to her, though she couldn't have known it. The fear and confusion that marked her face took hold of my heart.

I had met her a few times years earlier when she held herself regal, the wife of a successful lawyer who managed the real estate practice group of a large corporation. Back then she was self-assured, a picture of fashion and polish. The contrast between that woman and this same woman so many years later was especially merciless and stunning.

What a cruel disease Alzheimer's is, I thought. *He is a good man to keep her close to him in social situations like this and not exclude her.*

The hostess called the husband's name. He sat his wife down on the bench a couple of arm-lengths from me and headed for the hostess station. I wished I could remember the wife's name so I might help to calm her in his absence. I tried to put her at ease with my smile, to send the message that I wasn't comfortable in this large, noisy crowd either. But she just wanted out.

Everyone else was unaware as the wife got up and headed for the exit. I stood and grabbed someone's arm, interrupting him in mid-sentence, to ask him her name, tell him we have to get her. Then the woman's husband, trained by now to have eyes in the back of his head, ran toward the exit after her, took hold of her arm, and escorted her back to face the crowd she was fleeing from.

The trauma stays with me even after we are seated. I'm still mulling over the near escape and what I could have done differently. As former colleagues reminisce and chat about what is new in their lives, I remain too quiet. I attempt to appear interested in something across the room, study the napkin in my lap, look anywhere but into a person's eyes.

A lunch menu makes its way into my line of vision and I glance up with a thank you to meet the eyes of the Girl At The Cemetery. She is waiting our table. There are many waiters and waitresses and tables, but here we are, she and I, at the same table. We acknowledge each other privately with muted surprise and awkward smiles. I try to act normal. As if the earlier experience doesn't mean a thing. As if my son wasn't killed. As if this isn't the girl I just met crying at the cemetery whose last name is Ryan and who has Ryan's last photograph and is best friends with The Driver.

!MPACT BILLBOARD

"Oh, my God, there it is." I point through the windshield, above the highway and to the right, into the distance ahead. My insides turn to liquid weight and pool at the bottom somewhere. I forget to breathe.

It gets clearer as we approach. The faces first, three teenage boys. All innocence and opportunity. Then the words, "Please Slow Down, Someone Loves You." Then the messenger, "Mourning Parents Act."

Michael pulls to the side of the highway and brings the car to a slow stop. The billboard looms above us. Ryan's smiling face and the faces of the other two boys, full of optimism and dreams of the future, shine down on us. These boys look every driver who passes in the eyes. *Please Slow Down*, they beg. *Someone Loves You*, they promise.

I open the passenger door and swing my right leg out to stand. I want to look at the billboard with no barriers between us. No glass windshield of separation. It's a good billboard. Both the images and messages are compelling. Amber mirrors my action by opening the right rear car door and I'm suddenly alert to the danger.

"We shouldn't be here," I warn. "At the side of the highway

like this." I settle back down into the front passenger seat and close the door. "It's dangerous," I add, willing Amber to stay seated and close the rear door. She does.

"I needed a minute," Michael says.

We are all silent for a while. I twist my head to look at Amber in the back seat and see she's struggling to hold back tears. My poor baby girl. My first-born child. The one who taught me there is no love greater than a mother's love. The child I cannot protect from this grief. I reach back and pat her knee.

"It's powerful, isn't it?" I say, turning back to the billboard.

RYAN'S CROSS

I can do this, I tell myself again as the fear takes on a life of its own. I force myself to take deep, slow breaths. *Be still, my heart.* I hold tight to the steering wheel of the new-to-us Prius, assessing my ability to drive. The symptoms get worse the closer I get to The Cross, which stands erect at the side of the road where the car crashed. Just beyond Killer Curve. Where Ryan lay dying in a snowbank.

Traveling south, The Cross is on the right, up a little grassy bank at the foot of a sprawling sugar maple. I am approaching from the opposite direction that the car was traveling. From that other direction, The Cross marks the end of Killer Curve. I hope I am not having a heart attack.

I pass The Cross and pull into the driveway that serves the old white-washed farmhouse. There is nowhere else to park. *I hope you don't mind*, I murmur as I bring the Prius to a stop. I sit for a while, looking for any movement in the house or the opening of a door. Someone who lives here gave the kids permission to hammer The Cross into the ground at the edge of the tree line. Pat said the woman was very nice. *I hope you don't mind*, I mutter again as I grab the dozen white roses lying in the passenger seat and reach for the car door handle.

This is the place that straddles two worlds. The world to the south of The Cross held a vibrant teenager. The world to the north of The Cross cradled a dying boy. I step out of the car and scan the road, right to left.

Ryan was fine when he was there. At that point, he was alive and healthy and well. I circle my head to follow the road that leads to The Cross. But when he was there, all hope and promise were wiped away. A mere two hundred feet of calamity waiting to happen. And then, it was a snowbank that held my dying boy in its intimate embrace. *Were you cold? How long . . .?*

I shake my head to turn off my mind as I make my way to The Cross. There are signs that others have been here. Extinguished glass-jar candles crowd the base. There are wilted flowers, a washed-out ribbon, an accumulation of small stones. I remove the timeworn Christmas wreath that still sports a bright red bow from the intersecting arms of The Cross, set the bouquet of roses I brought with me against the upright stake, and tidy up by gathering as many of the burned-to-the-bottom glass candle jars as I can carry.

I press the fingers of my free hand to my lips and transfer a kiss to Ryan's fading name.

It is a small memorial. Yet a sacred place. One a mother cannot ignore.

FAST AND FURIOUS

⌘

*I*t takes no time at all for !MPACT to garner publicity and support. Three grieving moms sporting their anguish and emotion on the surface like a classy new spring jacket command attention.

Small victories befall us in quick succession. The Connecticut Department of Transportation is the first state agency to reach out to us. The then-Commissioner offered administrative support after she read a cover story about our high school program in the *Hartford Courant*. I am appointed to the Allstate Foundation Teen Driving Safety Advisory Board as the bereaved parent representative. We are a compelling force in influencing the adoption of some of the earliest GDL laws in Connecticut—passenger limits, cell phone restrictions, nighttime curfew, and increased classroom and behind the wheel driver training hours. We form solid relationships with members of the Transportation Committee as a result of our fervent advocacy. We just won't go away.

Representatives of Connecticut Children's Medical Center reach out to us and we agree to collaborate with them to educate state pediatricians on the risks of teen driving. We send information packets to physicians' offices and urge them to have the safe teen driving conversation with their adolescent patients. That affiliation results in the formation of the Connecticut Safe Teen Driving Partnership, which soon expands to include other stakeholders. We establish short and long-term goals. There is never time for pause because there is so much more to do.

And now. After a phone call made to the Connecticut Department of Motor Vehicles, and after a call returned, Connie, Janice and I find ourselves in audience with the Chief Communications Director in a conference room at the main office of the DMV.

Bill listens as Janice, Connie, and I, still deeply grieving and admittedly naïve in reliable ways to effectuate change in sprawling state agencies, share our experiences and loss.

"Daniel was an only child," Janice says.

"Joey was just sixteen," Connie says.

"Ryan is my only son," I say, keeping him current with my words. Ryan *is* my son. He always will be my son. "The baby of the family," I add.

Speed, we all say. *Passengers*, we all say. *Inexperience*, we all say. *Alcohol*, two of us say.

Through Bill, we beseech the DMV to get involved. "Car crashes are the number one killer of teens in the United States. It's a public health epidemic. These deaths are sudden and tragic and preventable."

"What, specifically, are you asking the Department of Motor Vehicles to do?" Bill asks.

We summarize what we have been doing on our own and with other partners. We emphasize our efforts to raise awareness, advocate for policy change, educate teens, their parents and the public. What can the DMV do? Lend its support and its weight to these efforts. The agency that grants teenagers the privilege to drive cannot ignore something this significant.

We leave the antiquated colonial brick building without a

commitment but with some optimism that day. We know the facts are on our side. This is a crisis. And the Chief Communications Director did listen.

MARJ

Ryan would have loved this day. The sun is bright, the temperature is comfortable with no humidity, and it's Friday. I can't suppress the sorrow for all the beautiful days lost to Ryan so I took a half-day off work and the only thing I can think of to do is go to the cemetery.

I admire the new Victorian-style sign as I approach the entrance, the attractive plantings in front of the black wrought-iron fencing. *You're making your mark,* I assure myself as I weave to the left to drive through the puddle that sits in the low spot in the road, and then right, through the stone columns. I look toward Ryan's gravesite, and my heart gives a little flutter when I see the SUV near Ryan's monument. *Someone's there.*

But no. It's Dominic's mom at Dominic's grave, two lots over. Dominic who died from a car crash fourteen months after Ryan.

It's awkward. I don't want to intrude, but I already know I can't drive away. By the time I stop the car, I'm not so sure who is intruding on whom. I am so used to this place being my own.

I can't quell the sadness as I walk the few steps from the roadway to Ryan's grave. The first in the row.

We greet one another carefully. "Hi," I say, daring to glance up at her. "Bad day."

"I know," she says. I watch a tear slide down her cheek. "Me too."

I say things I wish I can take back as soon as they leave my mouth, like it doesn't get any better and nothing helps. Who am I to tell her this? Perhaps it does get better over time. I don't know for sure. Things change. The recent history becomes distant history. We somehow cope, even as we don't know how we are doing it. We make dinner, do the laundry, feed the pets. We are deeply changed, but we try to pretend we are not because the people around us cannot comprehend it. Nor should they. Nor do we want them to. We protect them from it by pretending. Some say pretending is the key to surviving.

Maybe the pain softens over time. Maybe we eventually focus on the beauty of our children's lives rather than the tragedy of their deaths. Maybe we come to believe in things we never thought existed. Maybe with time, we find some facsimile of comfort.

I'm a mess at this, I think as I leave the cemetery. I didn't mean to layer my grief over hers. *I have fourteen months more experience as a grieving mom, and I didn't give her any hope. I'm sorry.*

I have a vision in my mind's eye of meeting Marj in this same spot over the course of our lives, until finally, we are much older and bowed, standing in the footprints of where we stand today.

Tending to our boys.

Bound together forever by our loss and this lonely little cemetery.

LONELINESS AND LAUGHTER

I plop down onto the hardwood floor of the high school volleyball court during a break, cross my legs, and stare up at the basketball that's been lodged in the ceiling rafters for weeks now. Michael, who runs the recreational volleyball league in town, is off on the sidelines managing this and that with other players. We resumed most of our pre-Ryan's-death social activities after some stretch of time. Although we don't host parties anymore. Or socialize as much. Or go out as often. And I no longer mingle and share stories and laugh with the others during volleyball breaks. I've forgotten how and I don't fit the way I used to. I'm more comfortable now in a room full of grieving parents or a legislative hearing or an auditorium full of teenagers than I am in this crowd.

You're too serious, I tell myself. *Very serious.* I wonder if anyone notices.

Occasionally someone will ask me how I'm doing. Usually Rich or Don, and sometimes Tom or Vern or Jim or Jeff or Bart or Steve. They are sincere. Concerned. Michael is attentive and gives me private indications that he's aware I don't feel quite right. A look, a touch, a question in his eyes: *Are you okay?* We often leave before the games are over now. Others have to pick up the slack by taking down the nets and bringing the box of volleyball equipment home with them and then back again the following Tuesday evening.

I wonder how long it will take for someone to decide they should free that basketball from the clutches of the ceiling when Michael's laughter brings me out of myself. It draws my gaze to the side of the court where he and a group of other players are smiling and bantering.

I still startle when I hear genuine laughter springing from Michael's throat, bursting through his mouth, lighting up his eyes.

PUNCH IN THE GUT

Something like panic tightens my stomach as I reach for the television remote to turn up the volume. "Four teenagers were killed last night in a car crash in Bristol," the announcer says. There are images of a silver mangled car on the television screen. In the background is a cemetery. I want to turn away, but I can't.

"Oh, my God."

Michael leaves whatever he's doing in the kitchen to stand and stare at the television beside me.

It is not the names but the ages of the kids that sink in first. Sixteen, seventeen, sixteen, nineteen.

"Oh, my God, those families." I know what is to come.

The sick feeling in the pit of my stomach intensifies as I try to figure it out in my head. *Who was driving? They shouldn't all have been in the car together. That's dangerous. Very dangerous.*

"They were all in the same car?" Michael asks, reading my mind. All the learning I've been doing on factors that contribute to the high incidence of teen deaths resulting from motor vehicle crashes has served to educate him as well. He knows the danger of a crash rises dramatically with each added teen passenger.

"We need to strengthen the GDL laws," I say.

The three of us moms—Connie, Janice and I—have been rabid in our efforts to save young lives. In the time we have been together, !MPACT has expanded to include other grieving parents and young people who have been affected by these tragedies. Ryan's friends Melissa and Sarah have joined us to share their experiences in our presentations. And Nikole, who miraculously survived a crash that left her critically injured in high school, has also started presenting with us. On top of everything else, I wonder if we have the energy to do more.

Yet we must. Teenagers and their parents do not necessarily understand the risk of teen driving, or the factors that lead to the high incidence of injuries and fatalities. We still have a long way to go to educate the public and get optimum laws in place to introduce the novice driver to the driving experience in a gradual, more controlled manner. Sometimes kids didn't obey the laws already in place. Sometimes they don't even know what the laws are. Sometimes parents let convenience trump safety.

It's complicated. Very complicated.

"This happened in Bristol?" Michael asks.

Oh no. I have an inner dialog with myself. *When did we last present at Bristol High School?* About a year and a half ago, I think. *What grades?* I don't remember. My starkest fear is that one or more of these kids might have taken part in our safe teen driving program. That we had an opportunity to make a difference in their lives, but just that one chance. That we may have failed.

With an eerie intuition, as if he were reaching into my head, pulling out my thoughts, Michael asks, "Have you ever presented at Bristol High?"

The phone rings. I expect it to be Connie or Janice or a reporter or Bill from the DMV, who is in regular touch with us on these issues now.

I leave Michael's side to answer the phone rather than his question.

SOMETIMES THERE ARE NO VALLEYS

I flick the light switch to turn on the kitchen lights. They don't respond. Again. It's intermittent. Damn, I don't have the energy for this. Find an electrician, make an appointment with an electrician, meet with an electrician. *Ryan would have been able to fix this if he were still alive.* It's a spontaneous thought, but familiar. Four years, nine months, and six days ago he was an apprentice. He would probably be a master electrician by now. I miss my construction buddy.

When the kids were growing up, we purchased, renovated and sold a number of foreclosures. We owned five houses at one point and referred to them by their street numbers to keep them straight. 17. 60. 99. 104. 128.

As we tackled one renovation project after another, Ryan grew skilled right along with me. Envisioning what might be, calculating cost and material, and executing a plan. We framed walls and built decks and installed siding. He appreciated the thin, chiseled neck of an Estwing hammer.

Amber had better things to do, like reading and daydreaming and nurturing plants and animals. The most sensitive among us, it's ironic how it was always Amber who found the injured bird or duck or squirrel. A recuperating animal would join our family for a while until it was nursed back to health and then released into its own environment. Sometimes they didn't want to leave, like Scout the squirrel who would go charging up a person's leg as if it were a tree trunk to rest on someone's shoulder. And Cackle the grackle who even as a mature bird would take a bit of food from a person's hand or roost nearby and chatter as if in conversation. Amber lent a hand in construction sometimes, but not because she wanted to.

One summer Ryan helped Michael and me shingle the roof of our lakefront home. It was our third but largest roofing project. I tested him as we stood on the upper side of the property, looking at the rooftop.

"What do we want to do first Ryan?"

"Install the drip edge."

"And then what?"

"Lay the soldier course."

"How do we want to treat the valleys?"

"We want to weave them."

"Good. Exactly right."

"But there aren't any valleys," he added.

"What?"

"This house doesn't have any valleys."

"Hmm," I said looking the roof over. Indeed, there was no place where two parts of the roof sloped down to meet one another. "True. There are no valleys. This may be easier than I thought."

That was the summer I learned I never wanted to roof another anything, not even a doghouse, ever again. And it was the summer Nanauk learned how to climb a ladder up to the roof just as well as we could.

The sigh that escapes at the memory is involuntary.

You have to find an electrician, I tell myself unnecessarily. *Yes, I know.* But all my ambition is consumed with saving other kids from dying in violent car crashes, or renovating cemeteries, or spreading goodwill in Ryan's name through Ryan's Memorial Fund.

Other projects go unfinished now.

UNFATHOMABLE LOSS

"Do you think they'll do my make-up?" I ask Michael as we wait for someone to let us into a local television studio. I'm only half-joking because I really don't know what to expect.

"I don't know," Michael answers. "Maybe. Or maybe they don't care how you look. Just the anchor."

After a moment in which I wonder if he's saying I don't look good, and he probably wonders if what he said might indicate I don't look good, Michael adds, "But you don't need it. You look very nice." He snakes an arm around my waist and gives me a reassuring little squeeze.

There has been a predictable outpouring of grief and media attention following the crash in Bristol that robbed four teenagers of their lives and injured the others in an oncoming vehicle. I am thrust into the spotlight as a spokesperson for the tragedy. Me, who always shied from too much attention. Always the thoughtful observer, the sidelined player. How I've changed. I accept on-air interviews with local CBS, NBC, and Fox news channels, and off-air interviews with the written press.

Ronda, the aunt of sixteen-year-old Alyssa who was killed in the crash, sees my contact information on a newscast and emails me. She is grief-stricken and doesn't know what to do for Alyssa's parents, Amy and Dave. She doesn't know what to tell her own daughter, Alyssa's cousin.

We grow close as we talk regularly on the phone for what might be hours on end. Janice and I meet with Ronda, her sister Amy, and Amy's husband Dave at a restaurant. Ronda's piercing scream upon learning that Alyssa was thrown from the vehicle exemplifies the urgency. We agree more must be done. I have always said I don't want !MPACT to grow larger with new members because if it does, that means more young lives have been lost. Other families destroyed. But !MPACT keeps expanding.

Alarm manifests itself in the safe teen driving advocacy community. Yes, more needs to be done. We have worked tirelessly to get the protections we have in place now, but it's not enough. We need to do more.

Several weeks later there is another crash. A seventeen-year-old driver, his fourteen-year-old sister, his sister's fifteen-year-old friend, a vehicle towing a boat on a trailer, a box truck. Three additional teenagers robbed of their futures. More families shattered. When will it end? This unfathomable loss?

A grandmother of the siblings killed in the latest crash sees me on television and calls me.

"I don't know what to do with myself," Faith says, "and I don't know what to do for my daughter."

The urgency is further magnified.

There is no stopping us now.

A PRESS CONFERENCE, A PROMISE, AND A PEN

I see myself almost as Ryan would if he were watching from somewhere above me in the sky. He would see his mother standing behind the right shoulder of the governor of Connecticut, who is seated and poised to sign a new bill into law that will implement some of the most protective GDL provisions in the country. It might surprise Ryan how his mother has changed. Gaunt. Shoulders not so square. A tendency to bow her head. When she does look up, he can see the merriment is gone. But not the determination in her eye. She hasn't lost that determination.

It is a bright clear April day and this ceremonial signing is the culmination of four months of dedicated work by Connecticut's Task Force on Teen Safe Driving. The task force was established by the governor not long after the two crashes in the state that took the lives of seven teenagers. It was co-chaired by the Commissioners of the Department of Motor Vehicles and the Department of Public Health.

Many task force members are here, including representatives from the Department of Transportation and other state agencies, law enforcement, insurance, healthcare, education, and driving schools. I wonder if Ryan would be proud that his mother was appointed by the governor as one of the bereaved parents to serve on the task force. Perhaps. We worked very hard to assess existing laws, evaluate studies and programs, and develop both short-term and long-term recommendations for the adoption of a holistic, best-practices GDL program in Connecticut.

And now. Here we are, staring into camera lenses with the governor seated in front of us outside of a Connecticut high school preparing to sign into law the result of our months of labor. We've established friendships in our common goal that may last our lifetimes. There is Joe to my right, and Bill and Ernie off to the side. I steal a glance at Tim, to my left, who lost his seventeen-year-old son Reid in a crash less than a year and a half ago. He catches my eye and gives me a tight-lipped bittersweet smile. I return it. We've accomplished what we hoped for, but the cost was too high.

When it is my turn to speak, I conclude by turning my face to the sky and pledging for all to hear, "This is for you, Ryan." I had fulfilled a promise.

The governor then signs the new public act into law with an effective date of August 1 and hands me the pen.

PART IV
REFLECTION

In Memoriam

I used to
wander the house
searching for you,
lie on your bed
breathing you in.

I used to
stand at the window
waiting for you,
listen for the sound
of your coming home.

Even now,
these years later,
I find myself searching.
I find myself waiting.

PREPARING FOR THE PAROLE HEARING

I worry over Nova as I brush my teeth, choose the outfit I'll wear to the parole hearing, plug in the iron. Yesterday when Michael took Nova to the veterinary clinic to be treated for an intestinal ailment, the vet recommended she stay the night.

"We should call to find out how Nova's doing before we leave," I shout to Michael as I iron my blouse.

I can't stop my mind from the fretting—over Nova, today's hearing, the words I will say that I haven't yet formed. I can't rid myself of the angst of seeing The Driver again for the first time since the day the judge sentenced him—one year, four months and twenty days after Ryan's death. *What does he look like now?* The question slips into my mind before I can halt it. It's the same question that sometimes intrudes when I think about Ryan. *What does he look like now, my handsome boy, after five years, six months and twenty-seven days in the ground?*

I try to purge the thought and go back to thinking about endings and how all traces of Ryan are disappearing from this world. Some abruptly and some after a lingering while—his laughter, his energy, his scent. How this parole hearing marks another ending. But I won't let this world strip itself of Ryan so easily. I will broadcast to everyone in the hearing room how special and loved Ryan is. I'll describe the cavernous void he left behind. Ryan will live on in their minds.

The phone rings and startles me out of myself.

"Hello?"

"Hi, Mrs. Chapman?"

"Yes."

"This is All Creatures Veterinary Clinic."

"Hi. How is Nova doing?"

"I'm sorry," the woman says. "Nova passed away this morning."

Michael is beside me now. The woman on the other end of the phone continues talking as I hold the phone out to Michael, whose face has gone pale and drawn. I want to run but there is nowhere to go, so I take the few steps it requires for me to collapse onto the bed and bury my face in a pillow. Grieving this new loss. Another ending.

THE HEARING

I wept over Nova and what the world had thrown at us and what the world had taken away for the entire forty-minute drive to the prison in Brooklyn, Connecticut where the Board of Pardons and Paroles hearing was to be held.

"How can I not have known?" I asked Michael. "It didn't even cross my mind she might die."

"Neither of us expected it," Michael answered, his eyes straight ahead on the road. "It wasn't only you." His jaw muscles were tight and there was moisture at the corner of his eye. He sounded tired, took a deep breath, and sighed. Grief is so exhausting. I placed a hand on his thigh. Nova was his favorite.

Another regret is forming. As Michael was leaving yesterday to take Nova to the vet, I called to her. They were in the driveway, Nova ambling behind Michael, me striding to catch up behind them both. Nova stopped and turned her head to peer at me. We were standing in a narrow path between the car and the garden bed in the front yard. There was no easy way to walk around her like I wanted to, to nuzzle my face in hers. So I placed my hands on her back instead and told her she was a good dog. I would see her later.

But that was a lie. Unintended, yet still a lie. There will be no seeing Nova later. I wish we'd kept her home for that last night of her life.

Now, Michael and I are led into a secure room in the Brooklyn Correctional Institution. I'm not sure if it's an omen or a quirk in timing that on this day before Independence Day we are ushered into prison for deliberations that will probably result in another person being ushered out.

A uniformed officer seats us to the left of the aisle, facing a table at the head of the room where the parole panel sits—two men and a woman who will cast judgment.

The Driver's mother enters the room with the Girl At The Cemetery. The Girl At The Restaurant. They are escorted to seats on the far right. I look briefly and only once, not understanding the bubble of fear that rises in my stomach at recognizing the girl. We had shared private moments. Perhaps I thought she was mine.

Finally, The Driver is led in donning cropped hair and reading glasses, looking young and studious. A college kid with a bright future, one might assume if one didn't know better. I'm not surprised by the sympathy I feel for him. It's been there all along.

My thoughts keep drifting back to endings, even more magnified now that Nova is dead too. A boy and his dog no longer of this earth. It's just so tragic that everything has to end. My entire being sinks under the weight of the knowledge of it. My shoulders. My eyes. My heart.

The parole panel first questions The Driver, who says he has thought of "it" every day since he has been incarcerated. I get so hung up wishing he had called Ryan by his name instead of "it" that I can't absorb much more being said. At some point, one of the male members of the panel comments that The Driver looks like a nice young man.

Another member of the panel asks us if we have anything to say. Michael turns my way. Our unspoken understanding is that any last words will be mine.

I tell them I am not here to comment on whether they should grant parole. That I leave it to their judgment. That I knew this day was coming and yet I am so unprepared for it. That I knew The Driver would live to grow older, get released, experience milestones in his life, perhaps get married, have children and grandchildren. All the while Ryan lies decaying in the cemetery. Never growing older than nineteen.

"This feels like another ending," I continue. "I never expected all of these endings involving Ryan. Even their pets die. Ryan's dog, Nova, died this morning."

I am weeping anew now.

"I want you to know that it doesn't get any easier with time. Grief has descended on our family like a thick blanket we can't crawl out from under. It is always there. We are more serious, somber versions of ourselves. We don't laugh like we used to. We don't experience joy. We dread holidays. I avoid music. A certain song can throw me over the edge. I don't even grocery shop anymore. It's too hard. Walking by the foods that Ryan loved, the things I would have bought just for him. Reaching for the smaller carton of milk."

My words touch them. I see it in a varnished eye, a rapid blink, a gulp of water. My voice cracks as I continue.

"Our home doesn't have the energy it did when Ryan was alive. It's too quiet now. Ryan is and always will be our only son, the younger of our two children. Someone vital to our family is missing and has left behind a monstrous void. Someone we love mightily. Someone who loved us. Now there is one less person in this world who loves us. What do we do with all that love and Ryan no longer here?"

Everyone's head is lowered as I continue.

"Ryan had every expectation that he would have children and we had every expectation that he would give us grandchildren, give his sister nieces and nephews, give his nephew Kalum cousins. Ryan had it planned. He would have three children. But no—those children are lost to us too. They, along with all his other unrealized ambitions, lie in Ryan's grave with him. I deeply mourn those unborn children. What do I do with all those hopes and expectations of the future, with all of those dashed dreams?"

I am bawling without reservation. Michael wipes away his own tears and places his hand on my back.

"I worry more now and I experience terror in a way I never did before—when it's been too long since I've heard from my daughter; when I hear sirens; when my husband doesn't get home right on time; when we receive a phone call at an unexpected hour; riding in a car. Sometimes I feel the impact that killed Ryan. I didn't expect the sheer terror I experience so regularly now."

I look up at the three people who constitute the parole panel, knowing there is nothing pretty about my face at this moment. I let them bear witness to raw grief at its deepest and tell them that our family's sentence will not end with a parole hearing.

"Our sentence will last our lifetimes and the generations beyond."

ODE TO A BOY AND HIS DOG

We are the picture of a cliché, Michael and I, skulking under the cloak of darkness. The four-by-six-by-six-inch container I have clutched to my abdomen is heavy with the weight of its contents. We may be skirting some rules, but I am determined we're doing the right thing. Michael pauses at the road-side of Ryan's grave, spade hanging from his left hand. I walk the long way around to the bench on the other side, careful not to step on the boy, and take a seat.

The ground is planted thick on top of Ryan with descendants from our own gardens. This is our way of bringing home to him, as I had promised. The creeping phlox and lavender and moonbeam coreopsis by their mere presence forbid the visitor to tread on this spot. There's enough weight already on top of the boy.

How are we going to do this? The light of a summer night's moon reveals there is nary a spot for digging left.

"Poor Nova," I place the tin on the bench beside me and give it a little pat.

My desperate efforts to preserve everything about Ryan were successful only part of the time. I can preserve his belongings, but not his scent. I can preserve the cards and notes he wrote to me, but I couldn't keep his dog from growing older. I can't stop time.

"It's so sad," I raise my head to face Michael. "Isn't it just so desperately sad?"

I guess he considers my question to be rhetorical. The answer obvious. He responds with another question.

"Do you want to do it?" he asks, soft and tender. "Or do you want me to do it?"

I'm still lingering on the question I asked of him, thinking that the deed should not be rushed.

"I feel like we should have a moment of silence," I say. An unanswered question for an unanswered question. Tit for tat. "Like a service, or reflection or something."

He agrees.

I bow my head, close my eyes, and let the memories surface. They erupt as visions. I can see how Ryan used to carry Nova around like a baby, sometimes under his jacket close to his chest to protect her from the chill. She was small and frail as a pup. As Nova grew older and shed her frailty, the two wrestled like siblings and swam in the lake together. When Ryan was home, Nova laid at his feet or followed him around the house, never too far behind. She seemed always to be grateful to be in his presence. The Inseparables, I called them.

When Ryan wasn't home, Nova either was out with him, or she waited. She waited by the door. She waited in his bedroom. She stood outside with her nose pointed up the driveway and she waited.

"Remember when Nova almost drowned?" I look up to seek Michael's eyes.

He nods. "That was scary."

Although he was at work when it happened, the incident is stamped into our family's collective memory.

It was early winter and I let Nova out as I did every morning. Ice had formed on the lake that bordered the south side of our property, but it wasn't yet thick enough for ice skating. It was too soon for Ryan to make the ice hockey rink he and his friends shoveled out on the frozen lake every year. Not yet safe enough to ice fish.

Ryan got up and called for Nova. She didn't come running as she normally did, obedient companion that she was. He kept calling. I looked out of my bedroom window overlooking the lake and noticed a little black something in the ice about a hundred yards out. Struggling. It took me a good long pause to realize it was Nova's head.

"She fell through the ice," I shouted as I ran downstairs and grabbed the phone to dial 911. Ryan flew out the door, headed for the lake. I was a few steps behind him yelling, "No, Ryan, don't!"

I knew instinctively he was going to charge onto a sheet of ice that couldn't carry his weight to save his most faithful friend. Ryan kept running, hysterical, shouting, "It's okay, Nova. Hang on. I'm coming!" I kicked off my high heels to run faster, crying and shouting for Ryan to stop, finally catching him just a few feet from shore. I hugged him bear tight as he tried to pull away, told him help was coming, we have to wait for help. By that time, a neighbor had pulled out his rowboat and was sliding it across the thin ice toward Nova.

That story had a happy ending. A neighbor with a heart and a boat. A mother's fierce embrace. A tragedy averted.

"Remember how proud Ryan always was of Nova?" Michael asks. That elicits another memory—our shared birthday when Ryan was fifteen and I was forty-something. Nova joined in the excitement by jumping up on Ryan so that her forelegs rested on his shoulders, her hind feet on the ground, standing nearly straight up in the air. There was something gallant about her stance. "Mom," Ryan said. "Look at this." His face alight. "She's never done this before," he said, a suggestion of pride in his voice. "Good girl," he told her, petting both sides of her head. I shared in his delight, noticing that if Nova walked on two legs, she and Ryan would be the same height. She gave him a lick that covered half his face. "Good girl," Ryan said again, then wiped his face dry with his forearm.

Nova was three months shy of seven when Ryan was killed. Her boy. My boy.

I think back to how Nova and I used to run into one another as we wandered the house looking for Ryan. Sometimes as I stared out the window wishing Ryan home at his scheduled time, I'd see Nova sitting by the front door doing the same. Other times I'd go to Ryan's bedroom to lie on his bed and breathe him in, but find Nova had beaten me to it. We saw ourselves in each other's grieving gazes. We worried about one another after Ryan died.

Nova never recovered. She was a sadder version of herself after Ryan's death. We all were. It is as if someone pulled down the shades, leaving our lives a little darker. At first, Nova was restless. Pacing. Searching. Over time, she grew more placid. Resigned.

"I'll do it," I say, responding to the question Michael asked earlier that I had ignored. We make the exchange with outstretched arms over Ryan's grave. I hand Nova's ashes to Michael. He passes the spade to me.

I find a bare spot, top and center, drop to my knees onto the cushion of the creeping phlox straddling the coreopsis and dig. Not too far down. Just enough to accommodate Nova's urn. But it takes some time. A song erupts from my core—my yearning for everything lost expresses itself in unpolished melody as I work the rocky soil.

"Hush little baby, don't say a word, mama's gonna buy you a mocking bird . . ." The last notes are broken. Like a heart.

A dog belongs with his boy.

JANICE

"I just can't do it anymore," Janice says as she hands both Donna and me a sheet of paper across Donna's dining room table. I know it is a resignation letter. We've talked.

"With work and other things going on in my life right now, I just can't do it."

My heart plunges even though I knew this was coming. An organization like !MPACT does take its toll. Reliving the trauma. Trying to save other parents' children. Joey's family was the first to step away. Now Danny's mom.

"And I'm not sure how much longer I can be effective," Janice adds. "As a speaker, I mean."

We've talked about this too. When does the story get too old? When do the photos fade? When do the memorial videos become dated?

And when does a mom begin looking more like a grandmother than a mother?

Yet how can one disengage from something that has become a part of you? That defines you? We do have influence. We are saving lives. Our current focus is on federal legislation that will standardize GDL laws throughout the United States. We cannot stop now. I understand how others might have to walk away and leave that piece of their lives behind, but for me the investment is total. How do you wash your hands of this animal that is the substitute for mothering your son?

I will never leave !MPACT, I vow to myself as I assure Janice through the fear I feel at her leaving.

"I understand," I say. Because I do. "But for some reason, this scares me," I admit. Janice and I have seen each other through the thick of it. The deep grief, the reluctant acknowledgment—they are gone, truly gone, not away at camp, but gone—the need to change the world, carry our boys into the future.

"I know," Janice answers. "I'm sorry."

"That's all right, sweetie, it's hard," Janice's sister-in-law, Donna, says. "We understand."

Not long ago I sought out the Sunday edition of the *Hartford Courant* that held Ryan's obituary, concerned that the words weren't good enough. When I opened the paper to the page revealing Ryan's smiling face, it startled me to see Dan's photo as well. I don't know how I had missed it. "Did you know Ryan's and Dan's obituaries are in the same newspaper on the same day on the same page?" I asked Janice afterward.

"Really?" she replied. "Oh, my." Another thing tying us together at the hip. I don't want to let go.

"You're not leaving." I turn to Donna, who we now refer to as DD to distinguish her from the other Donna. She is the only founding member of !MPACT besides me remaining now. "Are you?" I wonder if she might feel it is time for her to move on too, being Danny's aunt.

Janice and I both study her, waiting for an answer. I realize I am holding my breath. After a pause, she answers, "I don't think so. No."

Her words bolster me. I pull my shoulders back. Sit straighter. "Okay, good." I release the oxygen that's been building in my lungs, turn to Janice.

"We'll really miss you," I say. "But just because you have to step away from !MPACT doesn't mean this is goodbye."

I prepare myself to accept this new loss.

THE ENVELOPE

The fear creeps into my chest and paces in circles before it settles in my stomach with a plop, like an aging dog that is planning to stay awhile. There is no shedding the weight of it.

The envelope sits on the highest shelf of the bookcase. It is no small envelope that one might stuff with a check to pay a bill. No, this is a large ten-by-thirteen-inch manila envelope, three inches deep, filled with all the documentation necessitated by Ryan's death. It holds photos and reports, billings and findings from the medical examiner, the state police, the DMV, the hospital, the surgeon, the probate court and private investigators. I remove it from the shelf for the first time seven and a half years after Ryan's death. Ninety months. His anniversary. Two thousand, seven hundred and forty days.

I dust off the package and stare at it a while, not moving. I have been wondering over the past week if I might be ready for this. Now I know I'm not. I wanted to reconstruct the day the state trooper came to the house and took Michael's statement. What had Ryan been doing in the hours leading up to the crash? Compare the statement with my own recollections. My memory told me there was so much more that report should have said.

Maybe I can just thumb through for the page with Michael's words and ignore everything else. I gather the courage to move, package still in hand. I have saved this mission for a time I would be alone in the house. I hold the envelope in outstretched arms away from my body as I make my way into the bedroom. Even though I am alone, I close the bedroom door.

Sitting on the bed, I remove the contents of the envelope, a tidy clipped stack of papers, and read the cover letter. It concludes with the line, "I will prepare an affidavit of closing of this estate." Words that mean there should be nothing left in Ryan's name. Finalized. Completed. Done. Gone.

I place my hand on the top of the pile and my nose begins to burn as I do battle with a sob, with time, with everything that leaves me helpless. And then I use my thumb to fan through the bottom of the pages, looking for Michael's name.

Other words assault me. Ejected . . . thready pulse . . . code red . . . black Honda CRX . . . passenger side impact rollover . . . LIFE STAR not flying due to fog.

Words I am not ready to see, things I'm not ready to know.

Why did I even think I could do this? I grab the stack of clipped papers to stuff them back into the envelope. A photo disengages from somewhere within and falls face up. It's a picture of the smashed car. I close my eyes tight from the image as I stuff it back into the middle of the package. But not before my mind registers that I see Ryan's shoe.

RYAN'S SHOES

I cannot stop thinking about his shoes. The shoes he wore the day I took what I thought was his last photograph. How he wouldn't walk through the snow with them, risk water stains on the fresh new leather. So I didn't get the picture with the backdrop I wanted. The lush green of the pine grove in our back meadow contrasted with the white brilliance of unsullied fallen snow. Instead, the photograph was taken on the shoveled brick walkway, with the front of our home in the background. Not the photograph I wanted, but one I treasure. Taken nine days before Ryan struggled for his last breath.

In the other photograph, taken eleven or twelve or thirteen days later by some investigating officer, Ryan is nowhere to be found. And there is only one shoe. One of those shoes he was so worried about protecting from the snow. In a mangle of metal, resting on its side in the crush of the front passenger floorboard. Waiting for its boy to come back and claim it.

Photographic evidence.

There once was a car. A car that was speeding down a winding country road.

There once was a boy. A boy who was meticulous with his shoes.

A CEMETERY COMMUNITY

The sun is spring bright and it tries to warm me but there is still a nip in the air. The concrete bench I am sitting on is reluctant to shed its winter chill. The protective length of my coat between us shields the worst of it. I place the roses on Ryan's grave and pull my lunch from a brown bag. A chicken taco, refried beans, guacamole, and salsa. This has become my habit now. I leave work at two o'clock, grab a late lunch to go from our favorite Mexican restaurant, eat lunch at the cemetery, and finish my workday from my home office.

I guess you've come a long way, I tell myself. Not that long ago I couldn't eat at all. But people were growing concerned. My body couldn't shed much more than the thirty pounds it already had since Ryan died. So, I've been trying to eat again.

Yet today, even the fragrance of some of my favorite foods doesn't bring on an appetite. My eyes are drawn again to the fresh earth of the newly filled grave one row over from Ryan's. It is the grave of the elderly man who lost his wife less than a year and a half ago. The man I was accustomed to seeing on a Sunday sitting in the fold-up metal chair he brought with him each time, waif-like, staring at his wife's headstone. Sometimes we sat separate and quiet. Sometimes we talked.

"She'd be mad," he once told me, "that I had the figure of a young lady engraved on the monument." I looked at the carving of the beautiful woman draped in a Kimono. "But that's how I think of her," he said.

I reach down for one of the roses I brought for Ryan, walk over to the fresh grave and carefully place it in the center. "He won't mind," I say aloud, thinking how strange it is that I now belong to this lonely little cemetery community. Knowing all these things about people I never would have known. I know this man loved and missed his wife desperately, to the point that he lost his own will to live. I know the woman whose grandmother raised her will bring gallon-size milk cartons of water each week during the growing season to nurture the roses surrounding her grandmother's grave. That she might pull a weed or water a thirsty plant where Ryan lies. And I know some people find it too hard to visit at all.

On my way back to Ryan's grave, I stop at Dominic's and take his unlit candle from the glass enclosure. I bring it to the car, grab a book of matches, always with me now, and light it. Then head back over to Dominic's, careful to walk around Ryan, careful not to step on Dominic, and place the lit candle back into its protective glass case.

"There," I tell them all with a panoramic sweeping of my head.

"Now you don't look so lonely."

A SMILE FOR !MPACT

⁂

*J*take a headcount of the people seated around the table. There are nineteen of us now. All members of !MPACT. All survivors of calamity. Moms and dads and grandparents and aunts and siblings and friends. Each with a horrific story to tell; the loss of a son, a daughter, both children, an only child, a niece, a nephew, grandchildren, a sister, a brother, a friend. The only gain, one another.

"*There are so many of us,*" I almost say aloud. But then my mind turns to the two co-founders not seated at the table.

"Okay," I say after checking the time on the wall clock. "Should we get started?"

We follow the agenda, talking about the high schools we've served, our fundraising activities, our awareness program. I provide a summary of what's being done at the federal level to pass standardized GDL legislation throughout the United States.

Eileen, !MPACT's webmaster, discusses the new web content she's uploaded. I notice Linda looks shell-shocked. That's how it is with new members. Normally we have meet-and-greet events in a more informal setting, but Linda doesn't yet know everyone.

I clear my head to listen closely to what Eileen is saying and pull out some hard copy screenshots I've printed from the website as Eileen discusses the updates. She's added several new images.

One, in particular, a photo collage, catches my eye. Eileen has grouped photos of a very attentive teen audience surrounding a center photo of me speaking into a microphone. The caption reads, "You could hear a pin drop." At first glance I love it, but a closer study of the audience reveals that the caption is inappropriate.

"Uh-oh." I feel my eyes widen and look up to see everyone staring at me expectantly.

I open my mouth to explain why we need to remove the caption when some unintended little noise comes out sounding somewhat like a throat growl and I giggle self consciously.

"These—" I attempt to explain, "photos—" My giggling intensifies.

Oh no, this is serious and I can't stop laughing.

Eileen chuckles.

I want to say that the caption has to be removed, but the dismay over the photo collage has turned to mild humiliation over an unfortunately timed throat noise, which has now turned to hilarity and I can't get the words out. I'm choking on my own laughter.

"That caption!" I exclaim. Now almost everyone at the table is snickering. Even Linda has a puzzled smile on her face.

And that alone strikes me as side-splitting funny, making things even worse. You can't capture more tragedy in a single room than what we represent sitting at this table, and here we are, all cracking up over an involuntary throat sound and my exaggerated response to it.

I take a deep breath and think back to the kids in those photos. The lingering and the hugs following our presentation. The reluctance to leave. The eagerness to communicate. The lyrics in the movement of their hands.

The memory sobers me. I steady my breathing. Force myself calm. This is wrong. I've got to redeem myself here.

"These photos," another deep breath. Then I finally manage to say two whole sentences at once. "The photos in this collage were taken at the American School for the Deaf. It's very creative, but we have to remove the caption."

Eileen's eyes go wide.

"They were a great audience. Remember DJ?" I ask the other Donna. "They didn't want to leave the auditorium."

DJ nods. "They lined up to hug us," she adds.

Everyone is serious again now. The meeting doesn't last much longer. Ronda and I walk out together. She looks at me with a puzzled expression.

"You know," she begins, then pauses. "I've known you now for over three years."

"Yes," I acknowledge, thinking that is how long her niece, Alyssa, has been gone. One of the four who died in the Bristol crash. Thinking that she is as stunned as we all are by the passage of time. How it creates more and more distance between us and our loved ones. How I still count time. Seven years, eleven months, and four days since Ryan was killed.

"And," Ronda's eyes well up, "I've never seen you laugh before tonight. This is the first time I saw you laugh."

Her words cause a moment of reflection. I had laughed since Ryan's death. I think back to the elevator incident with Marla and Austin. But, she's right. Laughter is rare. Very rare.

Then I realize that I haven't seen Ronda laugh before tonight either.

THE CHRISTMAS TREE FARM

The little girl is dancing and singing to her own tune, "We got a Christmas tree! We got a Christmas tree!" *Four years old*, I guess. Even though December 7 looms, I cannot help but smile as I hand her a candy cane.

"Do you like your Christmas tree?" I ask.

"Yep. My daddy cut it all by hisself but he let me help." Daddy is beaming as he watches from a few steps away. He shares his daughter's bright pink cheeks.

"Well then," I say, "it sounds like your daddy earned himself a nice hot cup of cider." Amber has it already poured and stretches her arm out to hand daddy the cup of cider. He is timid, but slowly steps forward and accepts the warm beverage.

"Thank you, ma'am," he says. A southerner.

Amber responds with, "You're welcome," and then catches my eye as she turns away. I can hear the thought in her head. "Ma'am? He called me ma'am?" I give her a raised eyebrow and a little smile.

"Thank *you*," I say. "Your daughter could brighten a dungeon. What a little cutie she is. Are you going to decorate the tree when you get home?"

"I want to—" he begins, then stops. Finally, "You don't

know how much this means," he says. "I lost my job and, well, things are hard. But this is a wonderful thing you do here."

"Well, thank you, but it's our pleasure. We enjoy it. Especially when we see the kids having so much fun."

"I heard about your son. That you do this in memory of your son. I'm sorry. This is just a real special thing you're doing here. It put things into perspective for me." I notice his eyes beginning to mist as he looks down, shakes his head and says, "Thank you very much ma'am." He tosses his empty cup into the trash can, then turns and gently reaches for his daughter's shoulder. The emotion catches in his voice as he says, "Com'on princess. Let's go decorate our Christmas tree."

By three in the afternoon we are almost ready to head for home. Amber, Kalum, and Melissa have left. The cider and candy canes are nearly gone. The last of the families have driven off with their trees. It's quieter now.

"Do you mind if I take a walk up the hill?" I ask Bob, the owner who established the tree farm decades ago.

"Not at all," he responds. "Do you want a ride up on the tractor?"

"No," I tell him. "I'd just like to take a walk."

"Do you want me to go with you?" Michael asks. "Or should I pack the truck?" He motions with his head to Ryan's metallic green Dodge Ram pickup that we weren't able to part with, now adorned with signs on each door promoting Ryan's Memorial Fund.

"Why don't you pack the truck. I'll just be a few minutes." I turn and walk toward the hill leading to the heart of the tree farm. It is snowing lightly and I don't think I've seen anything so picturesque as the hilltop covered with the green of the many varieties of Christmas trees and the white of fresh snow with a backdrop of snowflakes falling against the crisp blue sky.

I think back to the year I suggested to the family that we didn't have to make our annual trip to this very tree farm for a

Christmas tree because we had grown some evergreens on our own property that were mature enough to harvest.

"What do you mean?" Ryan had asked. "We have to go to Hickory Ridge to get our Christmas tree. It's a family tradition. That's where I'm gonna bring my kids."

"Well," I said, "there's no arguing with that." And off we all went to Hickory Ridge Tree Farm, trudging up the hill with a bow saw to choose the perfect tree.

Some time after Ryan died, we asked the owners if they would be willing to partner with Ryan's Memorial Fund to provide free Christmas trees to needy families in the area, and they didn't hesitate. "Yes, we would love to partner with you on that," they said. And now it's become a new tradition, rooted in the old.

The higher I climb, the denser the tree growth. I am surrounded now, invisible to everyone and everything but pine needles and snowflakes.

"It's a family tradition," I whisper, repeating Ryan's words. Then more audibly, "It's a family tradition." The tears burn my eyes. "Ryan, I hope you can somehow know we are carrying on our family tradition."

But despite some sadness, I recognize it has been a good day. We made people happy. I had smiled and shared a light moment with Amber. Melissa is still in our lives. It was a really good day.

Three days shy of eight years; ninety-six months; four hundred sixteen weeks; two thousand nine hundred and twelve days since I last saw my son.

TIMING

It feels like wind is rushing through my head. December 7. The anniversary of Pearl Harbor and Ryan's dying gasp. The worst day of the year.

All morning I have looked at the clock and said to myself things such as, *Eight years ago to the minute, The Phone Call.* And, *This is the moment he died.* And, *At this very second we were sitting with the funeral director.*

We went to the cemetery, laid the dozen white roses, judged the time left on the candle. We looked for evidence others had been there, thankful his cousin had left a note and a holiday spray, thankful someone else had left a pebble.

Now we are home again, doing the mundane. The things we would do any other day of the year, like check the mail. And there it is, the envelope, addressed to Ryan's Memorial Fund. It comes once a month, a $25 pittance of an obligation from The Driver.

As soon as I see it, I close my eyes and stretch my hand out to pass the envelope to Michael.

"Great timing," he says, beginning to open it.

"He must have known?" I say with a lilt at the end that sounds like a question. "That it would arrive today?" I turn away and place the rest of the mail on the kitchen counter, disinterested. "Why would he do that? Insert himself like this on the day Ryan died? Or maybe he didn't know? Maybe December 7 doesn't mean anything to him." Both possibilities are equally hurtful.

Early on the probation officer and I had agreed the checks would be sent to the probation office and then forwarded to us so there would be no direct contact. But that didn't happen for some reason, and I was too weary to follow up. So now he is in our lives. Each month we are reminded by this trifle, no more, no less, that he lives. A name added to his check informs us he's married. A child's play set in a yard across town hints that he has children.

"There's no shaking him," I mutter as I do the calculation that never adds up. A limited-term, monthly check for $25 and the value of Ryan's life.

I can't balance this account.

MAPLE SYRUP OR TAPPING THE TREE

*M*ichael and I trudge through the snow to the largest sugar maple on our property. I carry the rubber mallet and two sap buckets, taps and hooks inside, clamoring with each step. He carries the hand drill and the bucket lids.

It is the perfect weather for tapping. Cool nights when the temperature drops below freezing. Sunny days like today in which it rises above.

"How's this?" Michael uses the drill to indicate a location on the trunk about three and a half feet from the ground.

I place the pails at the foot of the maple, dig out the taps and hooks, and look at the tree for several seconds. *Elegant* is the word that comes to mind. The limbs of the sugar maple are swooping and graceful, like a ballerina's arms. "That's good."

We haven't tapped the maples since Ryan was killed. It used to be our first rite of spring, before spring actually arrived. Every February we would tap, then collect and boil down the sap into syrup through February into March.

One year we tapped a swamp maple just for fun. The swamp maple is the poorer cousin of the sugar. The one who lives on the other side of the tracks. A little rougher. A little less graceful. We kept the sap from the swamp and the sugar separate as we collected and boiled it. Then each person in the family tasted them both. "Which do you like better?" I asked. Everyone preferred the sugar maple syrup except for Ryan. "I like the swamp maple," he said.

After that, we always tapped the swamp maple for Ryan and made him his own separate batch of swamp maple syrup.

The memory draws my eye to the swamp maple as Michael finishes drilling the hole in the trunk of the sugar.

"That ought to be good," he says. I hand him a tap and one of the hooks to hold the collection pan in place. Michael lays the drill on the snowy ground and picks up the mallet. I can already see a little drip of sap threatening to escape from the hole he's drilled. He knocks the tap into place just in time.

We brought the two buckets to tap both sides of the one tree, but I cannot stop looking at the swamp maple as Michael finishes up by securing the bucket and lid to the tap and hook.

"Okay, where next?" Michael asks, picking up the drill and following the trunk to the opposite side of the sugar.

I grab the second bucket and walk toward the swamp maple.

Michael lets me get some distance away before he shouts at my back. "Are you sure?" he asks, reading my mind.

He's probably worried about all the trouble this will cause, I think. *Like what do you do with the swamp maple syrup when the boy you made it for is dead.* But I have already thought of that in the moments leading to now. I'll pour the swamp maple syrup into snow holes at the cemetery and make frozen maple syrup pops. Ryan will get his swamp maple syrup.

"How can we do one and not the other?" I shout back to Michael over my shoulder.

PROCESS OF ELIMINATION

~~~~

I'm grateful when Michael opens the front door for me. I plow into the house along with a stream of the March evening chill, the overstuffed three-inch hot-pink Cemetery Commission binder and matching spiral notebook in my arms.

Even though I'm feeling harried, Nanauk's absence nudges at my heart. She recently died from the same ailment as her sister, and I miss being greeted at the front door by a dog.

"How'd the meeting go?" Michael asks.

"Okay." I don't really want to talk right now. I'm feeling overwhelmed with meetings and responsibility. I'm also getting tired of long months of cold.

"Thanks for getting the door." I walk into the office and dump the contents of my arms onto the chair. Shed my hat and scarf and coat and gloves.

"I'm having a glass of wine." My raised chin and eyebrows ask if I can get Michael anything. He shakes his head.

Merlot in hand, I settle onto the leather sofa next to Michael, take a sip, and set the wine glass in the coaster on the end table.

"I have to let something go." The thought that's been with

me for a while now has formed into words, and the words are finally out. "I need to figure out what activities I can release," I add by way of explanation. "It's too much."

"I could have told you that a long time ago."

"I know." For some reason, I feel sad. "But it's hard."

"Process of elimination," Michael says. "What's most important to you?"

It doesn't require any thought. "Ryan's book." I don't try to hide the quiet disappointment in my voice. I've let other things interfere. Capital G raises its nasty little head. I raise my glass to toast it. Hear, hear.

Michael nods. He knows.

"But everything is important," I rebut, addressing both Michael and Capital G. I work it through in my head. *The employment that brings in a salary: a must. The volunteer work that saves lives: !MPACT. The other volunteer work that carries Ryan's name and enhances people's lives: Ryan's Memorial Fund. And the other volunteer work that . . . well . . . hmm. The Cemetery Commission.* Michael watches me do the internal calculation.

"But I volunteered for the Cemetery Commission *because* of Ryan," I say as if Michael had heard the words that were swimming in my brain.

"I know you did," he places his hand on my thigh. "But maybe you've already carried out your promises to him. You've accomplished a lot in the years you've served on the Commission. What more is there?"

Have I carried out my promises to Ryan? Maybe. I'll have to talk to Ryan about that. They plow the cemeteries now. We've established self-guided tours. We've held public workshops on gravestones and carvers, cleaning and repair. We've reunited ancient footstones with their corresponding headstones. We've installed attractive signage. The unnamed road leading to Coventry Cemetery is now officially Memorial Drive. We have a beautification plan. We created a contemplation area in Nathan Hale Cemetery overlooking the lake. We've invited the public in, and there is renewed appreciation in the community for the art and historical significance of the town's cemeteries. *Have I fulfilled my promises to him?*

"Maybe," I say to Michael, responding to my own silent question.

But the question Michael posed, "What more is there?" goes unanswered.

TEE OFF FOR TEEN DRIVING SAFETY

Ronda introduces me as a founder and the president of !MPACT, then hands me the microphone when I walk up to her with a hug. I speak, almost rote now, the woman who wasn't able to address a crowd when Ryan was alive without a rapid flutter of fear, constricted throat, hot flashes.

"!MPACT was formed by the families of three teens killed in separate car crashes within an eleven-day period and a twenty-five-mile radius of one another." I begin. "Since that time, our membership has grown to include other parents, siblings, grandparents, friends, and survivors of car crashes involving teen drivers. Tragically, there are far too many of us. Every person you see here wearing a yellow golf shirt is a member of !MPACT. Every one of us has suffered unimaginable loss."

!MPACT's Tee Off for Teen Driving Safety golf tournament is the organization's annual fundraiser. I talk about how the net proceeds help to offset the organization's expenses and tout the number of Drive 4 Tomorrow presentations we've made in the past year. As I talk I am struck by how far we have come and I wonder if I have already accomplished what I needed to with !MPACT. Perhaps I'm almost there.

I look at Mary, Ryan's cousin, who has joined us this year to help out, and I cannot avoid glancing at her belly. Still flat. A flood of tenderness and gratitude engulfs me.

She called a few weeks ago. "Sherry, I have something to ask you."

"Yes?" I responded not knowing what to expect.

"If it's a boy, I want to name him Ryan. Would you mind?"

"Oh, Mary." I couldn't breathe for a moment. "Of course not. I am honored. Ryan would be honored," I said, holding back tears.

Now Mary sits down at a table by herself and I join her.

"How are you doing?" I ask.

"I'm okay," she says. "Kind of tired."

"I'm really glad you're here," I tell her, meaning that and so much more. I wanted to thank her for the promise of a new child named Ryan to squander my love on, bearing a name that will once again signify life. But I didn't know how to put all that to words, so I just said, "Thank you," and gave her a gentle hug.

A DASH FROM COLOR

"It's beautiful, isn't it?" The saleswoman at TJ Maxx has spotted me admiring the necklace. I pull my hand away from the smooth turquoise stone almost guiltily.

"Yes, gorgeous." The necklace is chunky, colorful and bold. Along with the turquoise is sliced blue agate, aged copper and bronze. Like something I would have worn in another life. Before.

I realize my hand is now caressing one of the few pieces of jewelry I do allow myself to wear. The locket around my neck bearing Ryan's name and photo. A bit of his hair.

"Twenty-five percent off today," she chirps. "Do you want to try it on?" She removes the necklace from the small display stand on the counter and hands it to me. I pause for only a second before reaching out for it.

"The color combination is striking," I tell the saleswoman as I fan the necklace out on the flat palms of both hands.

Maybe it's time. It has been so long since I embraced color. At first, I wore black, only black, every day like a visible wound. In those first few months when it took such effort to get out of bed and move at all, I wore one of two pairs of black slacks. Every day. People noticed. I felt it in their glances. But I didn't have the energy to care. It took so much strength to do anything at all. Now I have a closet full of black, and I still wear it every day, but it's not so evident. I've mastered it so you wouldn't notice unless you were looking for it. And even then, maybe not. Like concealer on a scar.

The saleswoman angles a framed mirror in my direction and I turn to my reflection. To the mourning locket and understated stud earrings. I hold up the necklace I've been admiring and place it around my neck so that it covers Ryan's locket. I see the expression on my face change. The colors complement my skin tone. *It's so pretty.*

"Shall I ring it up?" the salesperson asks.

I hang the necklace back on its display stand. "No," I mutter. "I'm sorry." My reflection told me it was impossible. Impossible to don a beautiful piece of jewelry and leave the mourning locket behind.

"But I'll take this," I say walking over to a nearby display to grab an oversize leather bag stamped in floral. It captures some of the same colors in the necklace. I hand the purse over the counter to the clerk without checking the price tag.

Determined.

Exhausted.

Like I swam upriver to get here.

POSSIBILITIES

The conference room is so full that my colleagues are gathered down the stretch of the hallway leading up to it. I follow Jane through the crowd of coworkers lining the walls to see me off and wish me well as I start this new life. I will miss many of these people and our regular interactions. Others will fade from my life with ease.

It started with an email.

"Wow," I said to Jane, my cubicle partner at the time. "I can't believe this."

"What?" she asked.

"The company's offering an early retirement program. Check your email."

I skimmed through it again. Yes, I qualified, having been with the company for most of my working life. For more than half of my life. The realization startled me.

The smell of someone's lunch wafted through the air above us. When they planned the move from our previous offices on the 4th floor to the cubicles on the 6th floor, they told us that the open layout would provide additional needed space. It did, but the cubicles also subjected us to other people's habits and conversations and odors. Someone was having fish for lunch and it smelled like leftovers. I pulled a napkin from the top left drawer of my metal desk and placed it over my nose and mouth before swinging my chair back around to face Jane.

"Did you get the email?" I prompted through the napkin.

Jane turned from her laptop and nodded as if it was normal to see me smothering my face. "I wish I could take it," she said.

The napkin proved inadequate, so I tossed it in the trash can under my desk. "Me too," I admitted. Things had changed. Faye retired a couple of years ago, and the job was turning into something that required me to be constantly available.

"Can you?" she asked.

"I don't think so," I said, even as I began to fantasize about it. "I don't see how I could."

Later that afternoon I whispered to Michael through the phone. "I wish I could take it. Fourteen months of severance."

"Well, let's not just dismiss it out of hand," Michael said. "Bring the information home with you and we can look at it together."

"Okay," I said, somewhat surprised Michael was open to it. Like it was a possibility. This made me think that maybe it was. "Thank you," I said before placing the phone receiver back into its cradle.

On the eve of the final day of the acceptance period, we made the decision.

"All right." I sat staring at the screen of my laptop. "There's no turning back once I accept," I warned Michael, who was standing behind me.

I was both frightened and excited. I was too young to really retire, but we had made plans. The severance package from my salaried position would provide me the time needed to establish my own company, 1 Stop Genealogy, and work as a professional genealogist. I would have more flexibility to write.

"It's a good opportunity," he said. "Go for it."

I placed the cursor over the button that read, "Accept," and paused just long enough for the effect. After all, this was a momentous decision. Then I clicked the acceptance link and turned around in my chair to high-five Michael. We both had big reckless smiles on our faces.

"Congratulations, honey," he said bending down for a celebratory kiss. "You did it."

"*We* did it," I said, gauging my reaction. *Am I frightened? Relieved? Uncertain? My heart isn't racing. My stomach isn't clutching itself.* I decided it felt like relief.

I sent personal emails to my supervisor and Jane informing them of my decision and the deed was done.

It is Jane I have to thank for organizing the retirement party. She said it started small and grew to proportions she didn't expect. As I follow her through the crowd flanking the walls leading into the conference room, applause erupts. There in the far corner is Austin. There up against the wall is Marla. In the center is a conference table covered with celebratory items including a large personalized cake, wrapped gifts and cards.

"Thank you," I say to the room. I'm overwhelmed by it all.

People speak. Jane talks about how close we've become working in the same Intellectual Property & Technology law group for the past twelve years. She shares something she didn't know about me until recently. "She collects globes," Jane announces. "World globes from different historical eras."

A former supervisor talks about how we grew up together working in the International law practice group.

"Remember when we went to Bermuda for lunch?" I ask, recalling a day trip we took together for a board meeting.

"I thought that was one of our secrets," he responds to the resulting laughter.

Another former supervisor shares a story about a significant contribution I made to a multi-million-dollar deal when we were working in Mergers & Acquisitions together. "She knew more about their technology and systems than their own lead lawyer!"

I am overcome with gratitude for the crowd and the memories and the kind words, while at the same time feeling oh so ready to be moving on from this phase of my life.

PART V
RESIGNATION

In Memoriam

For eleven years now
grief has sat at our doorstep,
plopped down on our couch,
settled onto our shoulders,
bowing posture that once stood tall.

Grief flung me from the highest cliff,
hurled me toward the deepest crevice,
a free fall,
going down, down, down.
The question always,
when and where would I land?

Ryan, I want you to know that I've landed now;
and that I landed on my feet.

Grief still pummels me in the stomach
when I see a birthday card from
mother to son or
son to mother.

It still raises its head in a candle flame
that garnishes a Thanksgiving dinner table,
illuminating an empty chair.

Grief is a companion I cannot shed.

But Ryan,
I want you to know that I've landed now;
and that I landed on my feet.

ON INHERITANCE

A girl who cringes at the pruning of a plant will fall into a deep abyss of despair following the sudden death of her little brother. It will take her a long time to climb back. She will climb back, yes, but never to the place she was before. She will come back changed. She will eventually prune a plant with abandon, develop a brittle exterior to hold all the molten trauma and emotion inside.

Along for the ride in this family who goes plummeting to the depths and stays awhile is Kalum. Poor Kalum. A child not yet three when the deep dive begins, who loses his playful uncle and is forced by circumstance to shoulder the great grief of his immediate family. Even though the family tries to hide it. They try to pretend. He is not fooled. He takes responsibility. He can be found tugging at a lethargic arm, "Come on. Get up." Trotting over to someone with a book in his hand, "Read me a story." Grabbing a coat, "Let's go outside."

The memories seen through a clearer lens these years later are every bit as painful as any memory I embrace. We were the adults. We should have done better. And yet.

Even our nervous attempts to bring melody into Kalum's life at an early age were forced. We stopped listening to music. We stopped raising our voice in song. Kalum took the lead in creating the only music we could tolerate in our home through his years of piano lessons and guitar lessons and drum lessons.

We do what we can to make it up to that child now. But the damage is done. The grief instilled. Kalum is too serious. He is also brilliant and thoughtful and sensitive. Sometimes he is adolescent-boy reckless.

There are studies which have found that grief transcends the bereaved. That deep sorrow and other emotional trauma induce genetic changes in a person that passes on to subsequent generations. Epigenetic inheritance. Can grief be inherited? Does it insist on being remembered in the absence of the experience?

Will Kalum's children suffer the trauma inflicted on this family by the sudden death of a boy they never knew?

Please world, be gentle with Kalum and the generations to come.

COMPETING CEMETERIES

I'm tugging at a chest-high weed in the garden bed of a nearby grave feeling melancholy, wondering what happened to the granddaughter who used to be a fixture here. The premonition I had early on has come to fruition. Me, an older woman, standing at a lonely grave. I didn't realize I'd adopt all the surrounding lots though, looking for a wayward weed, feeling especially sorry for the dead who no longer get visitors. Although even with a visitor, even with a lit candle and plantings and blooms, it's lonely. And some former visitors are buried here now. Like the man with the metal folding chair who sat for hours at his wife's grave while I sat at Ryan's. And the woman who tended her husband's gravesite just across the roadway from Ryan. Sometimes she would park herself in her car and stare at his headstone. Now the headstone bears her dates too.

The ribbons on the marker of the twin baby boys draw my eye. They've not been forgotten.

I light Ryan's candle and lean into Ryan's monument from the side, careful not to step on him. I run a finger over the outline of Ryan's face, engraved in black marble at my shoulder height. I lean over further and kiss Ryan's etched lips. "I love you," I say, wiping my hand across the damp lip marks I've left on his face.

"It's your grandfather's anniversary," I tell Ryan as I walk around the mound of him to the other side of his monument and settle onto the concrete bench. "I was thinking of visiting him." I weigh all the implications while I deadhead the daylilies. Killer Curve. The Cross.

Decision made, I heft myself from the bench and again touch my fingers to Ryan's lips. "I'll be back," I assure him.

When I am halfway into the driveway at home, I push the park button of the Prius and get out of the car, parallel to where Michael sits on the riding mower. It's not unpleasantly humid for mid-August, but the perspiration has dampened the hair on my forehead. Michael stops the engine and watches me approach.

"What's up?" he asks.

"It's my father's anniversary," I announce when I get close enough to be heard without shouting. "I'm thinking of going to the cemetery." I brush the back of my hand over my brow.

"My father's cemetery," I add because it feels like clarification is required.

"Do you want to go?"

NO MORE CROSS TO BEAR

The quickening in my stomach feels like fear. *What are you afraid of? There is nothing to be afraid of,* I try to convince myself. It's not like Ryan can be ripped from us twice. That's already been done. I analyze my physical reaction to approaching The Cross, and Killer Curve just beyond. Traveling in the opposite direction of the car Ryan was in.

I busy myself by trying to focus on our destination. I've missed too many of my father's anniversaries trying to skirt The Cross. But there is no easy way of avoiding it.

"I want to stop at The Cross," I announce to Michael without turning to him. *Might as well confront this head-on.* As soon as I think it, my mind adds the word "collision" to the end of the sentence . . . head-on collision. I shake it from my head with a long, flat hum. My hands are clammy on the steering wheel, despite the cool and constant gust of the air conditioner. My peripheral vision informs me that Michael has turned his head to study me, so I stop the humming.

"It's been a while," he says.

The car seems to guide itself as it slows to a crawl and makes its way down the hill. It passes the overgrowth beyond the embankment where The Cross has made its home all these years. It then approaches Killer Curve to the driveway of the farmhouse where the woman gave permission to set The Cross that bitter December evening. I bring the car to a stop in front of the house.

"It's overgrown," I say, stretching my head to search for The Cross in the distance. "I don't see it. Can you see it?"

"Not from here." Michael opens the passenger door and gets out of the car, giving me license to do the same.

"I wonder if the same woman still lives here." I scan all the doors and windows of the sprawling whitewashed structure to see if someone bears witness. Michael and I walk together through the parking area, across the lawn toward the overgrowth. Michael reaches back to grab my damp hand when I trail behind.

"Sorry." I apologize for the dampness and feel the sweat beading on my upper lip, my forehead.

"It's gone." Michael stops walking. "It was right in front of that tree. It's not here anymore."

He's right. It's gone. Someone must have yanked it from the ground. Disregarding the words of love and loss, the faded promises to never forget. Maybe they dismantled it. Tugged the shorter horizontal piece of wood from the longer vertical section, raised a right leg, smashed the centers of the rotting boards over a thigh. Splintering a name in half. Tossed the fragments into the woods. Or maybe carried them to the trash barrel. Or used them as kindling for a fire.

I turn the ninety degrees it takes to face the spot where the road meets the slope of the property, hyperventilating. I understand the fear now, what this place does to me. It distorts time. It takes me from today and thrusts me into a night where a snowbank was the only thing that embraced Ryan on that last day of his life. It causes me to wonder what those moments were like. What he was conscious of. What he may have felt. What he may have known. The fear. The pain. I cannot turn my mind off. *Where exactly did he land? Oh, God, get me out of here.*

I tug at Michael's arm and we walk back to the car in silence.

It surprises me that the absence of The Cross feels like another loss.

NOTHING IS FOREVER

"He must be off probation," Michael says out of the blue. We are sitting in our shared office at our respective desks, backs to one another. Michael is working on the financials for Ryan's Memorial Fund and I am finalizing a genealogy research report for one of my clients.

"What?" I am absorbed with my own project and have no idea what he's talking about.

"He's not sending checks anymore," Michael says. "He must be off probation."

Okay, now I understand. The Driver. I had wondered if he would continue to send the court-ordered $25 a month to Ryan's Memorial Fund after it was no longer required. Maybe out of loyalty to a friend, or as an apology, or to be a part of something good in memory of Ryan.

My physical response feels like resignation. There is nothing I can do about it. Nothing left to wonder about or hope for.

"He's moved on," is what comes out of my mouth, and at that moment all my ambition seems to have moved on with him. I save the Word file on my MacBook. Make a written note of the time. Push myself from my desk, out of my chair. I walk out of the room, through the back door, and into the flower garden.

I close my eyes and point my face to the sky. Breathe in. Long. Deep. Breathe out. Again.

The sun is brilliant, the temperature comfortable. Songbirds sing harmony in the background, only taking center stage when you let them. A cardinal calls out to its mate. The mate responds. There is the coo of a morning dove. And then a painfully melodic song that is less common. I scan the branches of the sugar maple for the oriole.

The sky is the blue of the sky that was Ryan's favorite. From earth, it does look like a playground for angels on a day like today. Cotton balls of cumulus entertaining chubby winged cherubs. Teasing them with their changing shapes. *It's an elephant! No! It's a rooster!* I wonder why I still search for Ryan in the sky.

Well, he's done. I don't say it aloud because I don't want Ryan to hear me. Ryan would be hurt by this I think. *He did what was required of him and now he's done. Another thing involving Ryan ended. History. No longer current.*

Some things will stop, like a monthly check, and others will disappear, like The Cross. People will move on and that will force Ryan to move on, from a fresh memory to a distant memory to a forgotten memory. Until there is nothing. And that is when Ryan will truly die. When all the memories are gone.

"I won't let that happen," I say aloud. My commitment remains strong. "How much big is the sky, Ryan. My words will carry you. I promise."

The weight in my stomach has dissipated. I know the power of a mother's love.

FORGIVENESS

&

"What's the matter?" Michael asks, looking up from the biography lying open on his lap.

I realize I've been staring straight ahead, past him, through the window into the distance at nothing. A Hemingway I've decided to re-read lies face down on my outstretched legs, which are propped up by the coffee table that separates us.

"I'm thinking—"

Michael tilts his head expectantly as I search for words.

"I'm thinking about forgiveness," I say. But it's more than that. I make another attempt at an explanation. "About what remains to be forgiven. And what I have no standing to forgive."

"Hmm." Michael furrows his brow. "Heavy." He leans forward, removes his bookmark from the coffee table, and places it in the two-inch-thick tome he's been reading. He sets the book down beside him on the couch and waits for me to expound. But I haven't fully thought this through yet, so there is silence between us.

What I'm thinking is I've done a lot of forgiving. I've forgiven those who uttered early, misspoken words of comfort. The innocent. The unknowing. The person groping for an appropriate thing to say. I've forgiven a damp boot print on a precious photograph, a phone call from a persuasive friend. I've forgiven the sideways glances at the same black slacks I wore to work week after week following Ryan's death, the people who avoided getting into an elevator with me. I've forgiven those who didn't understand why I wasn't getting better. Those who have been impatient with me.

I've forgiven nearly all the wrongs or perceived wrongs done to me. What is left?

The wrongs done to Ryan.

Michael tolerates the silence. I make another attempt.

"I've forgiven the people who hurt *me* since Ryan was killed," I say. "But I think no one other than Ryan can forgive the people who hurt him. I can't do it for him."

It surprises me that this realization has taken so long to form. All these years. I feel lighter for it.

"What do you mean?" Michael asks.

"It's like if someone slaps me in the face, do you have standing to forgive them? For the wrong they did to me? I don't think so. I would have to forgive them because the injury is personal to me."

Michael bites his lip and raises his eyes to the ceiling in thought. It is a dilemma. I know. Great minds have struggled with the concept of forgiveness—when it is warranted, and who has the power to grant it. In our culture, we are expected to forgive. And yet.

How can I forgive someone for a wrong they committed against someone else? I can't. It is not mine to give. And therefore, it is not mine to shoulder. A profound sense of responsibility is lifted just by articulating my thoughts and recognizing the logic of it.

Only Ryan can forgive those who trespassed against him.

Therein lies another tragedy. A dead boy cannot bestow forgiveness. No one can bestow forgiveness on his behalf. There have been, and are, and will be so many actions and consequences in this world that can never end in forgiveness.

A DEAD BOY'S CLOTHES

What do you do with a dead boy's clothes? With the clothes in those overstuffed, extra-tough plastic bags that you couldn't watch your husband carry up to the attic one by one. The clothes that had to be removed from a dead boy's room to make way for the living, because how do you tell your first-born surviving child who moves back home that she can't have a bedroom? That there's no room for her, the child who taught you the might of a mother's love, because you have to keep her dead brother's room intact. You can't do it. And so. She moves in with a child in tow that you can't protect from your own grief, and then she moves out. And now you're wondering what you do with a dead boy's clothes.

Well, you start small. You climb up the attic stairs. You gaze at the bags. You plod back down the attic stairs. You do this again. And again. Until one day, you drag the bags down, one by one, every step acknowledging the momentous occasion with a resounding ba-boom, ba-boom, ba-boom. You set each bag in the bedroom long since abandoned. Close the door behind you for no reason. You peer through a clear plastic bag and you see a familiar print. The gray T-shirt with the American flag on the front. You touch it from outside the bag. Judge your reaction. "Are you okay?" you ask yourself. "Can you handle this?"

You open the top of the bag. Stare at another shirt he once wore. That oversized yellow T-shirt with the Sean Jean print on it. Dress him in it in your imagination. Remember his ready smile. His erect posture. You almost smile yourself remembering him wearing this shirt. But the pain filters in because that shirt was orphaned long ago. You lift the shirt to your nose and breathe in. Is there any scent left? You take in the musty smell. No. You cannot believe so much time has passed since you've seen your son.

For some reason, you cannot release that shirt. You hold it to your chest, rub the smooth of it on your cheek, trusting in your son's DNA to transfer from the shirt to your own body. You know there have to be invisible slivers of him in there somewhere.

You rifle through his neatly folded clothes, removing them from the confines of those heavy-duty clear plastic bags that kept them safe for a decade. Nearly safe, because nothing can reverse the mark of time. That is one truth this journey has taught you. The elastic in his boxer shorts has lost its stretch.

You sit in the center of the room and surround yourself with piles of his clothes. You create separate towers of folded jeans, long-sleeved shirts, shorts, sweaters; unfolding and refolding and stacking.

He liked name brands. Tommy and Playaz and Fubu and Polo and Clench and Enyce. But he was particular. He called Everlast, Neverlast. Baggy was in then.

When all the unfolding and refolding and stacking has been done, and there is nothing more to do, you lay your head on one of the piles of the dead boy's T-shirts, close your eyes, and let the resignation take hold.

What do you do with a dead boy's clothes?

You still don't know.

APPRECIATION

The cool breeze brushes my hair back from my face like a caress. It takes me by surprise to realize I am no longer doing battle with the wind. Looking up from my book to find the bird whose lyrical song I don't recognize, I wonder when that stopped.

Michael, sitting beside me in the other lawn chair, puts his book down on the table between us. "Pretty, isn't it?"

It is pretty. The fish pond with the cherub fountain, the stone patio, the surrounding flower garden. We built it ourselves. Each of the plants and flowers symbolizes something: motherhood, unity, grace, love, devotion. The flowers in the daylily bed are just past. But the blue hydrangea and the pink roses and white phlox beyond the pathway are in full bloom. Ryan's memorial garden. It was supposed to be red, white and blue symbolizing Ryan's patriotism, but the red roses bloomed pink, so it's pink, white and blue. Ryan would get a good chuckle out of that.

On the opposite side of the pond by the iron gazebo, the lavender and Russian sage and pale-yellow coreopsis still entertain the eye. I feel something like tranquility and take Michael's hand. "I love you." He gives me a squeeze.

I'm evaluating how I feel. Is it happiness? Not unfettered happiness. Maybe a soft and quiet sense of contentment? It is certainly an appreciation of the life that surrounds me. Of my own precious life. I wonder if my past dozen years represent a life well-lived.

"We have to finish that greenhouse though," Michael says, looking beyond the garden at the aluminum framing that has stood without glass for, well, years.

"I hate that about us," I say.

"What?"

"Our modus operandi. That we almost complete a thing and then we stop."

"We've finished quite a few things this year," he rebuts.

"Yeah." But I'm thinking about all the things that remain to be done.

"Well, maybe this is our year of finishing things."

MEMORY QUILT

After a month of walking past the closed bedroom door, after a month of sometimes stopping to open it a crack and peek inside. I did it. I opened the door wide. I walked into Ryan's former bedroom. I sat in the center of the floor surrounded by the folded stacks of Ryan's clothes. I re-examined each of Ryan's shirts. I chose eleven shirts that were special to Ryan and held special memories for me. Then I made a separate pile. The eleven shirts, along with a square photo of Ryan in the middle, will make up the twelve pieces of Ryan's memory quilt.

It takes me another few weeks before I gather the courage to remove the black-handled scissors from the antique transferware vase in my office that holds my collection of pens and bookmarks and other long, narrow things. To bring the scissors upstairs. To open the bedroom door, walk inside, and set the scissors on top of the pile of eleven.

The day is approaching. The day when I will cut eighteen-inch squares from each of the chosen shirts. But I know that once I mar those shirts, I can never get them back in their original form. And so. I am deliberate in my actions. What is more meaningful? The shirts? Or a memory quilt?

ADVOCATES

"I'm proud of you." Michael pats my thigh as the jet gathers the velocity it needs to rise into the sky, pressing our backs firmly into our seats. I can't talk during ascents and descents. The risk mutes me. How is it that sheets of aluminum tacked together like band-aids can form these flying machines that defy gravity? A disaster waiting to happen. When is the last time they redesigned these things, anyway? Sixty years ago?

Long moments pass before the engines relax their scream, the jet levels off. "Thank you," I respond belatedly. "That means a lot to me." Now I pat Michael's thigh.

It awed me to learn I had been chosen as one of fourteen citizen activists throughout the United States to receive a Highway Safety Hero award from Advocates for Highway and Auto Safety. Someone noticed. All those trips to D.C. for press conferences and meetings with members of Congress to advance federal legislation that will protect teen drivers and passengers. All those ascents and descents.

"And you've been there every step of the way," I turn to face the gray-blue of Michael's eyes. And those lips. *When is the last time I told him I love the shape of his lips?*

"Thank you for being there. And for being here. For sticking through it with me. It hasn't been easy, has it?"

"No. It hasn't been easy, but it was necessary. There aren't any shortcuts."

I ponder Michael's words. Was everything we've gone through following Ryan's death necessary? The frenzy, the sinking, the clawing at anything within grasping distance, clinging to whatever might keep Ryan current and the family afloat. I guess it was. The whole of the journey was necessary, and it continues. Yesterday I was lost in the depths. Today I am aloft in the sky. Where will I be tomorrow?

It's been an incredible year. !MPACT's tenth anniversary. National recognition and solid statistics on fatalities involving teen drivers evidencing a significant downward trend. I feel like I've done my job. I didn't do it alone, but I put my heart, energy, and soul into it. I could not have given more. By the time the plane lands I decide I'm a little weary after all these years, but satisfied with the accomplishments.

"We don't have a lot of time," Michael says, stuffing his cell phone back into his pocket as we wait at the luggage carousel. The reception to celebrate Advocates' twenty-fifth anniversary is scheduled to begin in two hours at the Liaison Capitol Hill hotel. Advocates will present the awards in an event at the Sewall-Belmont House and Museum the following day.

"True," I acknowledge. "The one fallacy we all live with is that we think we have time."

Michael turns to me with a thin smile and I can read his thoughts. *Leave it to my wife to take a simple statement and turn it into a whole school of thought.*

~

It is an oppressively hot day in June. The rear terrace of the Sewall-Belmont House is tented to keep the sun at bay. Strategically placed fans strain to usher the humidity from the pavilion back into the open air.

"I think I overdressed," I murmur.

Michael turns to me. "What?"

I decide I shouldn't complain. "It's a charming location."

And it is. A historic brick building on Capitol Hill with a private and welcoming garden and enough room for everyone to mingle. It's a hobnob of Who's Who. High-level officers and directors of advocacy groups; citizen activist award recipients such as myself; state-elected officials; both House and Senate majority leaders; Democratic and Republican congressional award recipients.

The woman with Advocates who is pulling off the amazing feat of arranging the order of awards rushes up to me. "You're next," she says and hurries off.

The gentleman who introduces me lauds my advocacy in promoting state and federal graduated driver licensing legislation. The last line of the introduction is, "Sherry is currently writing a book with the working title, *How Much Big Is the Sky: A Memoir of a Mother's Love and Unfathomable Loss*."

Even as I walk up the steps and across the stage to the podium where I am presented with a Highway Safety Hero award from Advocates, I wonder how I got here.

I wonder how the person receiving this award can be me.

WITH (YET ANOTHER) REGRET

I am confident I'm doing the right thing as I park the Prius in the lot behind town hall, open the rear entry doors of the brick building, listen to my footsteps carry me to the town clerk's office. I had a long talk with Ryan. And Michael. But even he doesn't know that I've chosen today to be the day.

"Hi, Susan," I greet the town clerk.

"Hi, Sherry." She walks to the front counter. "What can I do for you?"

"Well, first off, I'd like to congratulate you on your retirement."

We talk about her future plans, what she will miss and what she will not miss.

"I am making a significant change myself," I add. "Significant for me."

She looks at me expectantly, her face a question mark.

I place the single sheet of paper I've been clutching onto the counter. Watch her expression as she reads the first sentence. "It is with regret that I tender my resignation as a member and chair of Coventry Cemetery Commission."

She looks up, probes my face before looking down again to read more. She knows what this means. She too has lost a son.

"I have enjoyed the ten years I have served this Commission. It has been a pleasure meeting and working closely with other Commission members, town employees, and elected officials. Unfortunately, competing demands prevent me from dedicating the time this position deserves."

She looks up again, this time with glassy eyes. I want to tell her that I'm not abandoning Ryan. That we had a long talk. That I am doing this to make room for something else. Something I must complete before I die. Instead, I touch her arm and say, "It's okay."

"What a loss," she responds. "You've done a lot."

"Thank you." I am moved by her response. "I'll work with the Commission to assure a smooth transition." But I want her to understand, so I go on. "There are other things I need to do in this lifetime. I had to assess where I was spending my time and what I could let go. It was hard, but this made the most sense."

She nods her head. She knows that the Cemetery Commission was a lifeline for me. That I was carrying out a commitment to Ryan.

"We only have so many decades in our lives," I add. Since Ryan's death, I have contemplated the nature of time. Now I wonder how much more of it I might have left, and what I need to accomplish before I go. I've lived five full decades. I will forgive myself the first and second, but I have to make the most of what time is left. And how many years that remain I cannot know. Ryan taught me that. He lived only one full decade. Not quite two.

Susan lifts the date stamp from the countertop and pauses it over the resignation letter. "Are you sure?"

The steps I have to take after this run through my head. First, I should call Tom to let him know. Tom, who I met on the beach volleyball court the same day I met Michael. Tom who serves on the Cemetery Commission alongside me. And then I need to inform other Commission members. I hope they understand why I told no one in advance. I couldn't trust myself not to stay on if anyone beseeched me to.

I look into Susan's aquamarine eyes and nod. She date-stamps the letter.

"Thank you for your service to the town," she says.

AMBER

A fragrant oversized bouquet of flowers lifts me when I walk into the kitchen. The colors are cream and yellow and blue, a gorgeous combination. Hydrangea, yellow roses, Easter lily, peony, bluebells. And a note from Amber wishing me a happy birthday.

"Oh, my God. Michael, look at this. It's beautiful!"

"Wow," Michael responds as he enters the kitchen. "It is. Impressive." I turn to hand him her note. "From Amber?" he asks.

I nod my head as I dig for my iPhone from the purse that's still draped over a shoulder and select Amber's number. She picks up after one ring.

"Amber! Thank you. It's beautiful."

"Happy birthday," she says. The girl who dreads the day as much as I do.

"I'm so sorry we weren't home. I love it." It's clear she made the bouquet herself. Decided on my favorite flowers, blooms that would speak to me, carefully chose each stem, arranged them just right. She too knows how to communicate through flowers. *Thank you for understanding, optimism, rebirth, honor, humility.*

"I would have liked to see you," I add.

"That's okay," she says. "I love you."

She lifts the funk I've been in all day. Even though Ryan's Day is tomorrow, even though it is the day before Ryan's Day, it's been hard. Ryan should be celebrating his thirty-first birthday tomorrow. I tried to write, but the loss extended to words. I have no son. I have no words. All I have are numbers. Tomorrow will be eleven years, eleven months and eleven days since Ryan's death. A bunch of number ones. When Michael came home from work, I told him I needed to get out of the house. Let's go out for dinner.

"I love you too, Amber. Very much."

As I place my cell phone on the counter, I feel so relieved that tears of gratitude slide down my face. It has been a long, hard road, but Amber seems to be happy now, and that makes me happy. I am so thankful.

Michael has been listening to my side of the conversation. He walks up behind me and places his hands on my upper arms, kisses the top of my head.

"She's happier now," I say by way of explanation. "Doesn't she seem happier?" I turn to greet his eyes.

"She does," he says as he wraps his arms around me and pulls me close to his chest.

SOME THINGS HAVEN'T CHANGED

~~~

Michael's habit is to stop at the cemetery and replace the candle on his way home from his weekly grocery shopping trips into town.

"Any sign of life?" I asked him a couple of days ago as he pulled the vegetables from the reusable grocery bag bearing the logo for Ryan's Memorial Fund. *Rooted in Love. Growing through Giving.* He turned his head to look at me with a quiver of a smile on his lips, a question in the tilt of his head.

I got it then. He thought I might be making a joke, but he wasn't sure. I wasn't making a joke, yet couldn't help an awkward laugh.

"Poorly phrased," I said. "I mean visitors."

Michael shook his head. "No." He continued to unbag the groceries.

No, there aren't many visitors at Coventry Cemetery. Some spouses and siblings and descendants and friends. The parents are the most persistent. There are more of them now.

Today, the sole passenger in the car with me is a tall, blue, glass-encased candle similar to the others that accompany me to the cemetery between Michael's shopping trips. I turn left onto Memorial Drive, follow the familiar stretch of road to the cemetery, and swerve a bit to the left so the tires roll through the puddle. Tire tracks as evidence. I was here Ryan. Some things haven't changed.

But some things have. I see my influence. The black and white Victorian-style entry sign hanging from an ornate black pole is welcoming. "Coventry Cemetery," it reads, with the establishment year of 1978 centered beneath it. The matching black wrought-iron fence sections extending from the outside of each of the stone entry columns provide a nice backdrop for the raised flower beds in front of them. Only one observation gives me a bothersome nudge. The sign announcing the Coventry Cemetery expansion project is not plumb. "Please excuse our appearance" leans a little to the right. But I've stripped myself of authority to have it straightened. My consolation comes in the form of a reminder that the sign is only temporary. *As are all things in life. As is life. Let it go.*

Ryan's monument still stands taller than the rest, at over six feet high when you calculate the added height of the base. The headstone is bordered on each side by Hinoki cypress that hover over it, planted by Amber years ago.

The candle in the candle holder suspended from the shepherd's hook that has stood to the right of Ryan's monument for all these years has not yet burned out but is about to. Good. I've reached it just in time. I know how long a candle of this size burns now. On average, two days. But the elements play with me. A wind can extinguish a candle flame or hasten its burn. A lazy warm day makes for a lazy candle flame. I usually get it right, but not always.

The loneliness pokes at me extra hard today. The whole family is going to Martha's Vineyard for several days. Well, all but Ryan. And when we travel, there is no one to replace the candle.

MICHAEL AND ME

"I haven't felt this relaxed in a long time," I say, realizing that our strides match. Right, left, right, left. For some reason, I see an image in my mind of a straight-legged army march. *Where did that come from?*

As soon as we boarded the ferry, all worry was lifted. This is why we love it here. The island has this effect on both of us. We are lighter versions of ourselves when we are on the Vineyard.

I take in an exaggerated breath of ocean salt air as Michael and I make our way from the Lookout Tavern, down an alley toward the Inn. He squeezes my right hand in his left.

"Home away from home," he says.

I swing our joined arms with the next few steps in agreement, already thinking of making a return trip in the fall.

Kalum is off with Amber and a significant other on some biking adventure. We all have our favorite things to do on Martha's Vineyard. Amber and Kalum go their own way and we ours until we run into each other at the Inn or meet for breakfast or dinner.

With rare exception, we stay at the same Inn on the Vineyard in Oak Bluffs despite ownership changes over the years. It is a place known and familiar. Our activities are largely predictable.

First stop off the ferry is the Lookout Tavern, situated on the waterfront, for seafood and a cocktail. We will spend time on "our" almost private beach, swim in the Atlantic, take the bus to Vineyard Haven to browse the Bunch of Grapes bookstore, sit through an author talk if one is scheduled during our visit. We may travel down island to take in a performance at the Old Whaling Church in Edgartown and stop in at Edgartown Books. We never miss having lunch at the local restaurant that serves our favorite clam chowder. We might rent a Mini Cooper or a scooter or take a tour or visit John Belushi's memorial, or watch the sunset from Menemsha Beach. Last year we took a ride in the bi-plane. We read and we write.

"Ahh, we're here." I kick a small stone out of our path as we turn the corner onto the cross street.

After climbing up one level, Michael unlocks the door to the room and the cool air conditioning beckons us in. I plop on the bed and stretch my back. Michael joins me.

He brushes the hair from my cheek. Kisses my mouth, lingering, soft and tender. He raises his head and gazes into my eyes. I trace his lips with my finger.

"Have I ever told you I love the shape of your lips?" He inflates them a bit, then gives me a mildly embarrassed smile.

"Not in a long time," he says.

I cup his face with my hands and admire the ocean blue of his eyes. We press our cheeks together. I run my fingers through his hair. He caresses my neck, settles his head on my chest, unbuttons my blouse.

Somewhere, somehow, sometime, between then and now, between fits and starts and trial and error, we found one another again.

WHAT REMAINS?

So what remains of the boy, outside of the obvious? An aging truck. Some stacks of clothes. Memories that won't survive the people who carry them.

What happens when a hearty laugh becomes an echo? When a stride is broken? When a voice is silenced? What of the energy that is created with a life?

What of the air molecules that one expels while on this earth? What happens to those twenty-three thousand breaths a day? Those one hundred and fifty million breaths Ryan took in and then released for the nineteen years and not quite nineteen days of his existence?

What of the DNA that passes from a developing fetus to the mother who carries that child? The fetal DNA that can live on in a mother's body for her lifetime? Did Ryan's migrating cells pass through my placenta to lodge themselves into my own skin or bone or brain?

I've studied these things and I want to tell Ryan what I've learned. And so I do. I say it aloud and in my head and with my pen, because there is a chance he can hear me or somehow sense what I need him to know. I've opened myself to possibility.

There may be different planes of existence we cannot comprehend.

"Ryan," I promise, "I know these things are true."

The world still carries you. It embraces the immortal energy that was and is uniquely you. It distributes your breath in its atmosphere. It holds you to its bosom in ways we do not yet understand or perceive.

Your family and most treasured friends still carry you. You inhabit our hearts and memories and inspire our words and actions.

Your mother still carries you. As you developed in my body, you passed to me the most basic of elements that combined to create the irreplaceable you. DNA does not travel in one direction only. You reside in the tissues of my body.

And Ryan, the future will carry you. You will live on with these words. Sixty-two thousand written words born of the fruit of your life.

No blink of an eye.

No temporary candle flame.

But a mountain, an ocean, a universe of a life.

ACKNOWLEDGMENTS

This book reflects a journey that encompasses many years, and a significant number of people have touched my life in that time. I am deeply grateful to those of you who allowed me to share parts of your own lives where they intersected with mine.

In the time that this book was written, I was honored to work closely with other writers. Thanks to Tom and Doreen, who helped me to find my voice; and to my friends and fellow UConn memoirists, who helped me to hone my writing skills. I am blessed to have shared time and space with such brilliant people.

My love to Austin Soares and Marla (Rogers) Small. Thank you for always being there. And to Janice Palmer, Connie Jascowski and Donna Doucette. Thank you for helping me to find purpose. And to Melissa and Kellie and all of Ryan's friends who remain in our lives. Thank you for keeping Ryan current. And to !MPACT and the greater safe teen driving advocacy community. Thank you for your tireless work.

I am indebted to my beta readers whose feedback and suggestions undoubtedly strengthened my writing: Sonja Chapman, Ronda Guberman, Karen Sanderson, Marla (Rogers) Small, and Laura Stone.

Thank you to Mary and Dave for namesake Ryan. And to Regina and Chris for Rylee. And to all the parents of children who carry Ryan's name as a middle name. You make my heart swim.

I am beholden to friends and family who stood by me even as I mourned too deeply, and cried too hard, and sometimes fake-laughed too loudly. Thank you for understanding all those years when I couldn't answer the question, "How are you?"

More thanks than I can convey to my husband and first reader, R. Michael Chapman, who always had faith that this day would come. And to my daughter Amber and my grandson Kalum for everything. The three of whom, along with Ryan, are my deepest loves.

READING GROUP QUESTIONS

1. Following Ryan's death, Ryan's mother questions how she can survive without both of her children alive and well. Yet she does survive. What are the things that encourage her to continue living?

2. Ryan's mother expresses dissatisfaction with her words. Do you think she finally found the right words and word combinations to successfully convey the trauma of her experience?

3. The book is broken into five parts that roughly resemble the stages of grief. Each section is introduced with a poem. Do you feel this is an effective way to draw the reader forward?

4. At one point in the book, the author states, "Grief so resembles insanity." Do you agree or disagree? Why?

5. Ryan's mother finds solace in the belief that her son lives on in ways that cannot be understood. She derives comfort in the thought that Ryan's DNA may survive in her own body, that the thousands of breaths he exhaled in his lifetime left minute particles of him that remain in the atmosphere, that the energy

created by his existence lives on in some form. Can you understand why these facts give the author some comfort?

6. The author talks about the inheritance of grief. Do you believe that grief can pass from generation to generation in the absence of the grief experience? Why or why not?

7. The author clearly exercises literary license and enjoys wordplay. Identify some double entendres and unique metaphors encountered in the book.

8. The matter of forgiveness surfaces as a weight that Ryan's mother carries until she realizes or concludes that she is not responsible for bestowing forgiveness on behalf of her son. How do you feel about that?

9. How did the author's relationship with her husband develop throughout the book?

10. Do you think the author is happy at the conclusion of the book?

11. What about the book stands out the most for you?

Made in the USA
Middletown, DE
06 May 2024